Mirella was dancing a solo. Slowly, sinuously, rippling and quivering, she twisted her limbs around the air and gathered hunks of it, possessing it. There were wolf whistles. She silenced them with a flash of her eyes, and then began moving faster, more wildly, stamping her feet as if to impress her own heavy rhythm into the shapeless swamp of music. She whirled and undulated, shaking her sphinx's mane. Her enormous dark eyes glowed. Her nostrils flared, her raspberry mouth was wide open. She flung her body into shapes which on anyone else would have been mere contortions, but which on her were ciphers, full of hidden meaning.

It was as if she were presenting them with a message, a warning, Janet felt — a declaration of ancient power, dark and irresistible.

Fatal Attraction

IMOGEN HOWE

TWILIGHT™

WHERE DARKNESS BEGINS...

Published by
Dell Publishing Co., Inc.
1 Dag Hammarskjold Plaza
New York, N.Y. 10017

Laurel-Leaf Library ® TM 766734,
Dell Publishing Co., Inc.

Twilight® is a trademark of Dell Publishing Co., Inc.,
New York, New York.

ISBN: 0-440-92496-0

RL: 5.9

Printed in the United States of America

First printing—October 1982

Chapter One

The weather seemed to have gone crazy. The air was freakishly warm and everything—the crocus and daffodil bulbs, the succulents in the rock gardens, the grass, the leaf buds—seemed to be sprouting and swelling as fast as they could. You could almost hear the electric crackle of cells dividing.

It's great to have warm weather, thought Janet as she bicycled behind her boyfriend David and his twin sister Diane. But there's something weird about it, too. But then again, Janet thought, maybe it's just me. I've been feeling a little weird.

Janet wasn't used to being sick. There was something disturbing about her headache; it didn't just make *her* feel bad, but it attacked the things around her, too. Everything she wanted to enjoy today, like the weather, seemed sick, nasty, and mistaken.

Maybe exercise was all she needed. She'd felt so cooped up in school all day. It was wonderful to get out. As she pedalled away, she breathed in the soft fresh air. Just moving, feeling the warmth of the sun and the rush of air eased the strange pain in her head.

She followed David and Diane off the highway and up the long dirt driveway toward the old house they'd moved into a year ago. It was a fine Victorian structure: three stories high, with porches, gables, plenty of gingerbread, and a six-sided tower with a window in each wall. Such architecture was unusual in rural Connecticut, where most of the dwellings were modern or copies of either colonial houses or seventeenth century saltboxes. An old saltbox had once stood on this site, but it had burned down in the 1850's.

The driveway ended in a loop. They got off their bicycles and leaned them against the stone gatepost. David ran up the walk. He was in a kooky mood—probably brought on by the weather. He bounded up the porch steps, set his books on the railing, and lunged toward the door. He struck an exaggerated silent movie listening pose with his hand behind his ear and pursed his lips.

"Shhh!" he said over his shoulder, as his eyes popped in mock fright. "I think I hear a ghost!"

He held the pose. A small shadowy form appeared in the darkness of the screened doorway and said, "Give me a break David." It was the twins' nine-year-old sister Cindy. She was as pixyish, curly-haired, and green-eyed as they were. Amy Gray, Janet's nine-year-old sister, appeared behind her carrying a platter of freshly-baked brownies. Cindy held the door open for her and she brought them out onto the porch.

"Brownies! You kids are fantastic. How come you're home so early?" said Diane as she grabbed a corner piece and began munching.

"The boiler blew, so they sent us home right after lunch," said Amy.

"Who needs a boiler on a day like this?" asked Janet.

"Amy has been helping me move into the tower for the summer," Cindy went on without answering Janet.

"Already? This weather is just an accident, you know. It's bound to get cold again," said David.

"So what? I'll use extra blankets."

Janet smiled at Cindy. "I bet from the tower you can watch the leaves come out," she said. She was trying to ignore the pain in her head. The brownies smelled so good she wished she could eat one, but just the thought made her feel worse. She sat down on the top of the porch steps, took off her shoes and socks, and leaned against the wooden pillar.

David began to stagger like a ghost. Just watching him made Janet dizzy. He held his eyes in a blind stare and thrust his arms straight out in front of him. "Where are the brownies? I don't see any brownies," he cried in a blood-curdling voice. "Oops," he said as he stumbled into Cindy. "What was that? I just walked through something cold and clammy!" He took a long, loud sniff. "And what's that ghostly smell?" Zombie-like, he turned and groped his way toward Amy, who giggled and hugged the platter close to her chest. David reached out his hand and his fingers curved like monster's claws around the stack of brownies. He caught two in his claws and shoved both of them into his mouth. "Ahhh! Invisible brownies," he said as he chewed, "home-baked by the ghosts! You know the only reason I can taste them, Amy," he said as he wrapped his fingers around her neck, "is because I'm a ghost, too!"

Diane roared with laughter when she saw the look of fear in Amy's eyes. Amy tried to laugh too, but it seemed more important to her to back away from David. Noticing that her friend was trembling, Cindy pointed to her brother and said seriously, "Come on, David. There are certain things you shouldn't laugh about."

"Oh yeah, right, I forgot, my loving little spook of a sister and her crazy friends the ghosts. I hope I haven't insulted the other members of your family."

Cindy frowned without saying a word. She didn't like it when her brother made fun of her, especially when he teased her about something that was important to her. But because she was the youngest, she didn't know what else to do but back away and remain silent.

"Yeah, David, don't tease the little kids like that," said Janet. "It frightens them."

Cindy did not like Janet's tone of voice, but she knew she was only trying to help.

David focused his attention on Janet. "Well, look who's awake from the dead! What's keeping you so quiet today, anyway? How come you're not laughing at my jokes?" David held a brownie in front of her nose. "Want a ghostie brownie, little girl?"

Janet looked at it but shook her head. "No thanks." She and David had been going together for nearly a year now and they usually knew each other's moods pretty well. But Janet felt so out of sorts today that even David's teasing seemed to make her head throb.

"What's wrong?" he asked as he popped the brownie into his mouth. "Don't you feel well?"

"No," she said, bewildered. "I feel weird. My head hurts. I just want to sit here and not do anything."

"You don't feel well?" Diane asked, astonished. The Gray sisters were famous for never being sick.

"I feel terrible. My hair feels too tight."

"Well," said Diane, "you probably have what's known as a headache. Lots of people get them. It's a drag, but I assure you it will go away." She opened the screen door. "I'll get you some aspirin."

"Your hair is too tight, huh?" said David, picking up Janet's long glossy dark braid and weighing it in his hand. "It sure is heavy." He made her move down a step, and began massaging the back of her neck.

"Oh, that feels good."

"Poor baby," said David. He pressed gently with his thumbs along the base of her skull. "Sweet sixteen and never been sick. Welcome to the human race."

"Well," said Diane as she returned with the aspirin and water for Janet. "Now we have another reason to give a party. In honor of your first headache."

"First and last, I hope," said Janet, gagging a little on the aspirin.

"You're having a party? What were the first reasons?" Cindy asked.

"Well, for David's and my birthday, even though that was three weeks ago, and for our housewarming, even though that should have been a year ago," said Diane. "It'll be fun. A lot of our friends have never seen this place, at least not since we've been here."

"Yeah," said Cindy, in a tone of dreamy excitement. "Maybe some of them will remember the Dexters. Mrs. Wiggins at the library told me that all the little kids in town used to visit the Dexters."

"So when should we have it? It ought to be soon," said David.

"How about the Saturday night in spring vacation? That's in two weeks, right before we leave for Washington," said Diane.

"Hey, Janet," said Cindy. "Did my dad ever ask you if you could water the plants while we're away?"

"Yes, I told him I'd be glad to," said Janet, who at that moment couldn't imagine ever lifting a finger again.

"That's perfect," said David. "Who shall we invite? The whole class?"

For some reason at that moment, Janet's head throbbed sharply. She watched a sleepy wasp stagger along the edge of the porch roof.

"Now Cindy," David began sarcastically. "Be sure to invite your ghostly friends right away. We wouldn't want their feelings hurt, now would we?"

David was referring to Clayton and Catherine Dexter, the former owners of the house. Clay and Cathy were twins, like David and Diane. They were born in the house in 1888, and lived in it all their lives. When Clayton was a young man, he was to marry a beautiful woman when suddenly and without reason, she mysteriously died. After her death, no one ever saw the twins again. It was said that they withdrew into their house and devoted themselves to studies of plants and birds.

"Ghosts have feelings?" Diane asked incredulously.

"Of course they do," said Cindy. Sometimes her sister seemed very stupid. "That's what ghosts are made of—leftover feelings."

"I've heard that theory before," said David. "Where are you getting your information about these ghosts? Are Clay and Cathy still telling you stories?"

Cindy frowned at her brother. During the past year, she had become very fond of Clay and Cathy. During the recent months, Cindy had learned a lot about them by reading their diaries. They had never mixed much in society or politics, but they did like children. Clay wrote about lovely spring days when children were taken on bird walks or herb-gathering expeditions. In wintertime, children from all around would climb the half-mile path through the woods to the kitchen door. Once inside, they'd drink hot chocolate and listen to stories around the potbellied stove, while the snow melted from their boots and made puddles on the oak floor.

According to the journals, the last stop for trick or treat on Halloween was the Dexter house. Every year, three or four bands of witches, cowboys, skeletons, and gorillas would make their way along the dark driveway and head for the pair of jack-o'-lanterns glowing on top of the gateposts. Just beyond, the monstrous silhouette of the house, closely guarded by tall trees, loomed against the sky.

Once past the jack-o'-lanterns, everything would be dark—except for the glow of firelight in the front living room window. But the eeriest thing of all was the third jack-o'-lantern that stood alone in the six-sided tower. As soon as they spotted it the children would bunch together and walk as a single unit up the steps. After a brief moment, one daring soul would reach up and knock on the big front door. It would creak open, and the children would be relieved to find their elderly friends and not the spooks they imagined would be there. After gathering apples, home-made cookies and candy, and pennies, the children would put on their masks and troop back into the darkness.

Why was it always scarier to go away from the Dexter house than to approach it? Cindy wondered.

"The Dexters sure were a crazy family," mused Janet. "There was such an air of mystery about them, nobody seemed to trust them. But people said they were always nice to children."

Cindy thought Janet must have been reading her thoughts. "Old people especially didn't seem to trust them," continued Janet.

"If only we could find that second journal," Cindy said, "then we'd know."

"Oh no, here we go again with the diaries," moaned David.

Cindy frowned again. She had taken an interest in Clayton and Catherine Dexter from the moment her family had moved in. When the Sperrys bought the house, it had been standing alone, silent and empty, for four years. Each of the Dexter twins had died on a cold and chilly November night, within two days of each other. The house had been willed to a nephew who, four years after their death, decided to get rid of the trembling old place. The Sperrys had heard about it from Calvin Armstrong, a local real estate agent.

"Remember that story your father told us about the first real estate agent who was asked to show them the house?" Janet touched David's arm and giggled a little. Cindy looked up, surprised. She wondered again if Janet could tell what was on her mind.

David and Diane laughed together. "Oh yeah, remember Dad saying that the old guy seemed to age thirty years right before their eyes? It wasn't until Mr. Armstrong explained about the 'ghosts' that Dad understood what had made the first agent tremble so much."

"The mystery of the Dexters," Diane wailed,

trying to imitate a howling October wind.

"Well, you have to admit," Cindy remarked matter-of-factly, "there is something very mysterious about what happened to Clay's fiancée."

"Yeah," said Amy.

Janet nodded her head. She remembered her father telling her the story of the Dexters one evening a long time ago. Just before Christmas in 1906, the Dexters engaged a young woman, an orphan named Margery Smith, to act as governess to their youngest children. Margery and Clayton, who was then a vivacious young man of eighteen, were taken with each other, or so people thought. But that May, Clayton met Vera McNulty and fell in love with her. Within a day of announcing their engagement, Vera fell ill and died and Margery disappeared. No one could explain the fatal tragedy.

"What ever happened to those diaries, Cindy?" Janet asked.

"I still have One and Two, but Volume Three is missing, and that's the one that would tell us all about Vera and Margery Smith!"

"I wish we could find it," said Amy. "The one thing everybody wants to know about . . ."

"Everybody?" David and Diane laughed together. "Speak for yourself little one," said David.

"I for one have more important things to do," chimed in Diane. She entered the house, leaving David and Janet with Amy and Cindy.

Cindy sighed and shook her head. Why couldn't David and Diane be more like Janet? Although no one was surprised when Cindy took an interest in the story of the ghosts, for she was imaginative by nature and loved to read stories of the supernatural, they did find her fabulous conversations with Clay and Cathy rather funny.

"I guess we should thank old pinchy-faced Mrs. Wiggins for getting you involved in all of this nonsense," David said sarcastically as he wrinkled up his nose in imitation of the school librarian.

"She's been very helpful to me, David," Cindy was firm. When Mrs. Wiggins had discovered that Cindy was interested in the tragedy that surrounded the house, she immediately loaded the little girl's arms with old leatherbound notebooks. They were Clayton's private journals which he had kept from the time he was fourteen until just before he died. Mrs. Wiggins had taken charge of them, as directed by his will. Now she had given them to Cindy. She also had shown Cindy an oil portrait that Cathy had painted of Vera. Cindy had been fascinated by the energy and humor in the beautiful face.

"Mrs. Wiggins told me," Cindy continued, "that she felt Clayton would have liked me and would have wanted me to have them."

"I wish we knew where the last volume is," sighed Amy.

"Me too," said Cindy. "But Mrs. Wiggins says it wasn't with the rest when she came to pick them up. She looked all over the house. She thinks Clayton must have burned it."

"I'll bet it's here somewhere," said Janet.

Diane poked her head from the door frame. "Has anyone seen my science notebook? I left it right here on the hall table."

David stood and twisted his face into an ogreish grin. "It's the Dexters! The Dexters have swiped it right out from under our eyes."

"Ha-ha," said Cindy.

"I can't wait to see how your ghostly friends behave at our party," said David. "Even if we wanted to, we couldn't keep them away."

"Not true," said Diane. "I've heard you can leave a bowl of warm milk out for ghosts if you want to keep them off your back. Is that true Cindy?"

"Ha—I bet they'd rather have a bowl of flaming brandy," said Janet. Everyone laughed, except Cindy.

"C'mon," she said to Amy, who wasn't laughing much herself. "Want to come up to my room?"

"Uh-uh—it's too nice out," said Amy uneasily. "Let's go swing or something."

"But I thought you wanted to see if—" Cindy began, then cut herself off.

"Go look by yourself," Amy said, getting mad. "I'll go see if Sue and Jimmy are home."

"Hey," said Janet. "If you two are going to fight, could you do it some place else? I don't feel up to listening to you, and we've got things to talk about."

The phone rang. Cindy jumped up and ran into the front hall. She called, "Some girl for you, David." They heard her feet thumping as she ran upstairs.

Reluctantly, David got up and went inside.

When he came out again, his face wore an odd expression.

"Who was it?" asked Diane.

"Oh, that new girl, what's-her-name," he said.

"You mean Mirella?" said Diane. "What's she want?"

"She said she'd lost the homework assignment for French," said David as his voice trailed off. He seemed embarrassed. His eyes held a faraway, cloudy look. He sat down again on the top step next to Janet, propped his elbows on his knees, and rested his chin on his folded hands.

Janet and Diane exchanged glances.

"She's indoors doing homework on a gorgeous afternoon like this, huh?" Janet said, unable to keep the sarcasm out of her voice.

"She gives me the creeps," said Diane.

"Me too," said Janet, gratefully. "She gives me a headache."

"That's dumb," said David. "How can you dislike somebody you don't even know? She's new and she's shy. She needs a little help, that's all."

"Shy my eye," said Diane.

"I suppose you're right," Janet said. Privately, she agreed with Diane, but she didn't want to be jealous unless it was absolutely necessary. She managed to smile at David and ran her fingers through his curly hair.

They heard Cindy galloping down the stairs. She burst out onto the porch, looking pleased and excited.

"Hey, Amy, want to go swing?"

Amy, who had been busy making some ants crawl over a stick, jumped up.

"Sure!"

"Don't be late for dinner, Amy," Janet said feebly.

"I'm never late," Amy called over her shoulder as she and Cindy ran around the house.

Janet reached around behind her, found her shoes and socks, and began to put them on.

"Don't go," said Diane.

"I've got to," she said. "I feel really awful. I've never felt this way before."

She stood up. David stood up too, and put his arm around her.

"I'll walk you to the road," he said.

"I just feel so dizzy . . ." Janet's voice tapered off as they headed down the driveway. "I've never felt this way before . . ."

Chapter Two

Janet coasted down the two-mile hill from the Sperrys' driveway to her own. Her bicycle tires sizzled through the shallow stripes of melted snow and frost that flowed across the road.

As she looked around, she marvelled at how recklessly the plants seemed to be shoving themselves out of the ground. At this time of year they ought to lie low, she thought, or tomorrow they'll find themselves cut short by March's pale sword.

And yet, she reflected, worrying about the weather is a big waste of time. I should know better, after all those discussions with David. She smiled as she remembered one particular talk they'd had last summer . . . They had gone to their favorite spot beside the brook, where the water usually slid thickly down a smooth rock and collected into a quiet brown pool. It was just the right kind of pool for cooling your feet in. But for several weeks there had been no rain and on that day, the rock slide was dry. Instead of a pool, there was only a puddle in a cake of dried mud.

They sat down on the bank. The air was dry and still.

"Look at this!" David said. "These woods are absolutely crisp. The reservoirs are shrinking. The lawns are like corn flakes. Dad's crying about his tomato plants. The papers are full of alarms and precautions about a drought. Everybody seems sure that everything is going to dry up. It really irritates me."

"What do you mean?"

"Well, every year there's a 'bad thing.' This year it's a drought, the last couple of years it was the caterpillars, next year, it'll be too much rain. But things always turn out okay, whether we worry or not. Why can't people realize that? I just hate fuss and worry!"

"David," Janet said "I agree it's easy for life to bounce back after a little drought like this. But what if it got like the Oklahoma dust bowl? Or what about volcanic eruptions, famines, wars—what about the Holocaust? Millions of people murdered, or their lives completely ruined? How can we say there's nothing to worry about?"

He looked at her, a spark of anger in his green eyes.

"I'm not saying that terrible things don't happen," he said quietly. "Obviously they do. I'm saying that worrying can't prevent them—it can only make them worse. Because life can't be destroyed. It can be loused up, for sure, but it always wins. Why can't people accept that, and trust it?"

Janet stared at him. At that point Janet and

16

David had only been going together for a few weeks. They were just beginning to find out why they were so attracted to each other and felt so comfortable together. And this is the main reason, Janet had realized. How often she'd thought the same thoughts he had just expressed—yet she'd always kept them to herself and figured she must be a freak. In the society she knew, anxiety was almost an obligation. People would sneer at her if she went around saying life couldn't be destroyed.

Was David the companion she had always longed for—the one she could share her secret optimism with? She tested him cautiously by giving voice to her own doubts.

"I don't know," she said. "It's all very well to say that *life* can't be destroyed, but what good is that to *me*? I want to live forever. Sure, leaves die and fall off, and new ones come out in the spring. But what good does that do the old leaves that are dead on the ground? If I die, and at the same time a baby is born, you say great, look at life going on—but that baby isn't *me*. I want *me* to come back."

"But that's the point! What if it *is* you who comes back in the new baby? What if the little green leaf we see in the spring *is* the same leaf that turned brown in the fall, only in a new body?"

Janet gasped.

"Don't you ever feel that you've lived before?" David continued, his voice low and excited.

"Yes!" said Janet, in the same tone. Then, a series of scenes, like a pack of picture postcards being riffled, had flashed through her mind. A dusty alley lined with tin shanties that flashed in the sun somewhere in South Africa . . . the porch of a brightly painted house on the edge of a Ukrainian wheat field . . . floorboards under her feet, the smell of sweaty costumes, fake swords clashing, an audience laughing raucously . . . through it all she looked into David's eyes, and found in them deep, unbarred love, comradeship, and a certain knowledge that he was part of those scenes—that they'd been together through many lifetimes, and would be together for lifetimes to come. Overjoyed, she smiled at him. He leaned over and kissed her.

She said, "We don't die. We live each life as well as we can, and when the body we live in wears out, we let it die and make a new one so we can live a new life. We can even do it together— we don't have to worry about being separated."

"Right." They lay down on their backs and looked up into the trees. David went on. "And you know, the plants understand that! They don't mind dying every year. Not even being eaten by caterpillars first thing in the spring."

"Do you really think plants are aware of themselves, the way we are?"

"Absolutely! Why should we think they're not?" He looked ruefully at the twig he was twirling. "Plants, rocks, insects—everything! I think we treat other creatures like lifeless *things* because, first of all, they look so different from us, and second of all, we have no idea of how to talk to them. But they're people like us—individuals with awareness and senses. They must want to live

18

forever, same as we do. Only they don't just wish—they *know*. So they're willing to let their bodies die. They don't worry and fight and take pills, the way we do."

"You know what?" she said. "I think that if there's really such a thing as evil, it stems from being afraid to die, from thinking that when your body dies, *you* die. Because if you believe that, you're going to want to preserve your body somehow, in order to save your soul. Which is impossible." She paused. "It would be like a candle flame trying to rebuild the wax it had just melted." They both laughed. "The laws of the universe just don't work that way. So you'd get desperate. And desperation is what drives people to do evil things."

"Trouble is," said David, "most people don't dare believe they even have souls." He laughed dryly. "Maybe the schools should have a required course in reincarnation."

"Ha!" Janet snorted. "That'll be the day."

Shortly after that conversation, Janet thought she'd never be afraid or worried again, that she couldn't possibly lose that feeling of trust in her own soul. But she did lose it. She didn't forget, of course, and neither did David. It was their secret discovery, a bond between them. But the magic, the immediacy of it, wore off. Soon she found herself worrying about homework and war and what would become of her, just as she always had.

Now, riding through the queer, warm weather, she told herself not to worry about the plants.

19

Even if it did get cold again, they would be just fine.

But she was having trouble believing herself. It was as if a piece of a puzzle she thought she'd solved had fallen out and disappeared, leaving a jagged hole through which dark, inexplicable misgivings scrambled, like insects through a crack in the wall. What right had she to say everything was okay? Nothing really bad had ever happened to her—yet.

The Grays lived in a colonial-style house in one of the older, more spacious housing developments. When Janet arrived, she hoped to catch her mother at work in her studio, but the lights and radio were turned off and her mother was nowhere to be seen. Maybe she just went out to catch what she could of the beautiful weather, Janet thought. No one else was home. Janet slowly carried her books upstairs to her room and closed the door behind her.

She dropped the heavy load on her desk. She knew she should do some homework before dinner, but she felt strangely exhausted. She thought that she might feel revived if she rested for a few minutes on her bed.

As soon as her head touched the pillow, the pain in her head banged against her temples. She couldn't keep her eyes open under its weight. When she let them close, her mind turned into a pond. The thin scum of nightmare, just partially seen, partially heard, and partially tasted, began to spread across her head. As it did, it spawned nasty apparitions that multiplied and fattened and swam toward her, sneering as they moved. She backed away, but they pressed closer and closer, until they were about to crush her against the back wall of her skull. "STOP!" she screamed to herself.

But when her eyes opened, the afternoon sunlight lanced into them and struck that double target of pain buried in her brow. She moaned. There seemed to be no comfort, no escape. She folded a corner of her white bedspread like a bandage, and laid it across her eyes. It filtered the light so that she was able to rest with her eyes half open, keeping both the pain and the stinking demons at bay. Before she realized it, she slid into a trance.

Janet saw herself on her back in the bottom of a small white boat which was tied to a wooden dock at the edge of a lake. The lake water was blackish-green, viscous, with a sickening swell to it— unnatural for such a small body of water. The lurch of the boat rolled the pain back and forth behind her eyes. She tried to believe she was safe as long as the boat stayed tied to the dock and did not drift into the middle of the lake.

Through the trance, she heard the front door of the house open and close as people came home— first her mother, then Amy. Janet heard Amy slam the front door, call snappishly to Mrs. Gray, and run upstairs where she slammed the door to her bedroom. A few minutes later her father's car drove in, and the garage door closed with a rumble. Mr. Gray entered the house quietly and went straight to the kitchen. Janet heard his deep laugh, and his footsteps, slower and heavier than her mother's. All the while, the white paint of the boat was smooth under her fingers, the slow waves rolled her back and forth, and the smell of the stagnant water coated the back of her tongue.

They'd call her for dinner soon . . . she blinked herself home from the trance. She could tell it was now dusk, from the fading light in her room. Sitting up carefully, she shielded her eyes with one hand, and with the other turned on her bedside lamp. Its soft light didn't hurt too much. She got up, washed her face and combed her hair, and went down to the kitchen.

"Oh, there you are! I wasn't sure if you were home," said Mrs. Gray, setting a hot casserole on the kitchen table. She smiled at Janet, then looked at her again, frowning. "Honey, are you okay?"

"I don't know," said Janet. "My head hurts."

Mrs. Gray touched her daughter's forehead. "You don't feel feverish. Are you hungry?"

"I'm not sure. Let me give it a try." She sat down at the table.

Mr. Gray stood at the counter tossing the salad. He turned around and with his eyebrows raised, gave Janet a long, playful but concerned look. "You sick? That's unheard of. I won't have it," he said as he dried his hands. He gave Janet a hug with one arm, and kissed the side of her head. Then he put the salad bowl on the table and went to the foot of the stairs to call Amy.

Amy clumped down the stairs the way she always did when she was mad. As soon as she came into the kitchen, it was obvious that she was in an awful temper. Her chair squawked as she pulled it out. She dumped herself into it and scowled at her plate.

"What's going on here?" said Mr. Gray. "Don't tell me you're sick too!"

"No, I'm mad at Cindy," said Amy. "She's getting to be a drag."

"Why's that?" asked Mrs. Gray.

"Because all she's interested in are those stupid ghosts."

"What ghosts?" asked Mr. Gray, although he already knew.

"She thinks Cathy Dexter hangs out in her room."

"The tower room, right?" said Janet. "That's a fantastic room."

"Yeah, it's a neat room all right, but it's creepy. She just moved back in there for the summer today." Amy lowered her voice dramatically. "Cathy slept there in the summertime, too. And you know, that's the room Margery Smith jumped out of. You know what Cindy says? She says Cathy visits her there, and *they play checkers*. She's got a checkerboard set up. Every day, she moves a piece and then goes away, and when she comes back, a piece on the other side has been moved. She says Cathy moved it."

"Was this checker game going on while Cindy was in her winter room?" asked Janet.

"It sure was. You should have seen her today, carrying the board up to the tower like a precious relic, being so-o-o-o careful not to let the pieces slide out of place."

23

Janet wanted to laugh, and Amy caught her smothered giggle. "It's not funny!" she said furiously. "Cindy's my best friend, and either she's going bats or, well, what if she's telling the truth? What if there really are ghosts? Can ghosts be trusted? They might drive her insane, or throw her out a window or something!" Tears spilled down her cheeks.

"Now hold it," said their father. "You've been letting those old stories get to you." He reached out and gently rubbed the back of Amy's head. "Don't worry, sweetie," he said. "There can't be any ghosts, you know. I'm sure Cindy's okay. She's probably playing a joke on you."

"She is *not* playing a joke! She really means it!"

"Well, she does have a wild imagination. Maybe she really does believe in ghosts," he said as she buttered a roll. "But something imaginary can't hurt anyone. Can it? Give her a little time—she'll lose interest in the whole thing sooner or later."

Janet rested her face in her hands. Something about this conversation was making her head hurt more. She felt she couldn't eat. "Excuse me," she said, standing up. "I have to go lie down."

Mrs. Gray stood up, too. "Honey, you're as white as a sheet," she said, feeling Janet's forehead again. "Still no fever. You feel kind of cold and clammy, though. Sure, go lie down. We'll keep your dinner warm in case you feel better later on."

Janet went up to her room and lay down on the bed, leaving her bedside lamp on in the hope that its mild light would keep the nightmares away.

The conversation about ghosts had made her feel panicky. There was something worse on her mind, though—a recent, unpleasant memory which she needed to think about. It might even be the cause of her headache. She drew a deep breath, closed her eyes, and allowed the image to take center stage in her mind.

Mirella.

Was that what it was? It couldn't be. She didn't want it to be. But the recollection touched a nerve so sore that her head felt a fresh throb, and her stomach twisted.

The nightmare began at lunchtime the day before yesterday. She and David had been on their way down to the cafeteria, holding hands as usual. David had just started to tell her a joke when he stopped and she felt a shock go through him. Then she saw why, and a jolt coursed through her own frame.

At the foot of the stairs, leaning against the wall, had stood the most awesomely beautiful young woman Janet had ever seen. Her preppy clothes— a pale yellow oxford cloth shirt and gray flannel skirt, dark blue cardigan draped around her shoulders, charcoal knee socks, and penny loafers— looked incongruous on her voluptuous body, which was as perfectly proportioned as a Greek vase. It was statuesque, ripe, at ease with itself. Her thick, pale blond hair was brushed back in a wavy mane from her sphinx-like face. Her enormous, slightly slanting dark eyes were a smoky, purplish-brown color and looked across wide, luscious cheekbones. Her skin was absolutely flawless, velvety, almost iridescent. A slight smile parted her full, raspberry-pink lips and sculpted her cheeks into a delicately sexy suggestion of a sneer. The tip of her tongue was just visible, and rested lightly on her lower teeth. She was gazing at David and there was no mistaking that lethal, triumphant hunger in her eyes.

Janet's heart landed like a stone in the pit of her stomach. Why is this happening? she wondered. It isn't fair. Nobody should be that beautiful. She took a quick sideways look at David. He was blushing. As they came to the foot of the stairs and crossed in front of the girl, he ducked his head and compressed his lips. Janet tried to shoot an icy glance into the eyes of the intruder, but it missed its mark. The single-minded gaze of this person refused to turn away from David long enough to be challenged.

When they passed her, Janet asked, "Who was *that?*"

"New girl," said David. "I met her this morning. She's in my French class. I think her name's Mirella, something like that."

"Oh really," said Janet. Then, to counteract the sarcasm in her voice, she gave David's hand a squeeze.

From then on, the sight or even the thought of Mirella drove despair like an axe into Janet's guts. *Why bother getting up in the morning?* she'd think. Life was over for her.

But Janet knew this didn't make sense. What was it about Mirella that made her feel so crazy?

Janet had never considered herself a jealous person. "What is it about Mirella that makes me feel like I can't breathe? What makes me feel like I'm dead just when I think about her?" she wondered out loud.

It seemed to Janet that Mirella waylaid David everywhere. She knew exactly where to find him at any given moment. She could corner him outside his classes, on the stairs, near his locker, and all the time she'd be effortlessly alluring, gazing at him knowingly, lazing up to him to ask him to do her a favor.

When Mirella had turned up later that afternoon in Janet's history class, Janet thought she'd at last have an opportunity to challenge her, to let her know how important she was to David. But as she'd done before, Mirella completely disarmed Janet by simply ignoring the challenge. She was invulnerable.

Janet could not figure her out. Mirella obviously didn't care about school. She merely occupied her chair. Maybe she was a little dumb. Quite possible, but somehow Mirella even turned ineptitude into an asset. She was perfectly self-possessed, never apologetic. She asked endless questions and favors of everyone, especially David, if he was around—and he usually was—or else of the person closest at hand. Wrinkling her mouth into her minimal, mocking smile, Mirella would walk right up to someone and say, "Hi. Can I borrow a pencil?" "I lost the homework assignment. Can I get it off you?" "Excuse me, which way is the

27

library?" "When did he say we're supposed to hand it in?" "Hey, David, I broke this. Do you think you could fix it?"

She asked these things in her husky, expressionless voice, and everyone always complied with her requests, even if they didn't want to. It was the strangest thing about Mirella. Somehow she made you feel that she was never really asking. She was *ordering*.

Today, for example, Mirella had been particularly annoying in her attentions to David, and Janet had found it harder and harder to stay calm. At the end of history class, Janet gathered up her armful of books and made for the door as fast as she could. She wanted to get as far way from Mirella as fast as she could. But there was a traffic jam at the doorway. While she stood waiting impatiently, she felt a loathsome touch on her arm.

She turned and there was Mirella, smiling her contemptuously sexy smile. She moved up close, uncomfortably close, and gazed into Janet's eyes. Janet backed away until she found herself pressed against the doorjamb, but Mirella continued to come toward her.

Mirella lifted her long-fingered white hand and pulled a long dark hair off the shoulder of Janet's tweed jacket. She rolled the hair between her finger, then helped herself to another. It seemed like an unconscious habit—she gathered two more while she spoke.

"Can I ask you a huge favor?" she said. "I didn't quite catch everything he said. Could I borrow your notes? I'll give them back to you after study hall."

"Sure, just a minute," Janet heard herself say. She put her books down on the nearest desk and fumbled through her notebook for the pages Mirella wanted. Why am I doing this? she had asked herself. I hate this person and besides, I'll probably never get my notes back. But it was as if Janet's hands were out of her control. The more she struggled for an excuse not to lend Mirella her notes, the faster her fingers flipped through the notebook.

"Thanks a million," said Mirella. And she disappeared into the crowd, leaving a trail of turned heads behind her.

I feel as if I'd been mugged, Janet thought as she watched her go. She smiles that way to mock your helplessness, she thought. She knows you'll go along with her. She knows you're afraid of her. She looks at David so smugly because she knows she's got him.

It was just at that moment that she first noticed the pain in her head. It felt like two sharp-edged discs, no bigger than dimes, but very heavy and buried in her forehead. Every breath she took seemed to rush up into her nostrils and hit the discs, fanning them until they glowed red hot. There was tightness and pressure at the back of her head. She wanted to let her head fall forward and close her eyes, but something warned her to stay alert and resist the temptation.

Of course Mirella didn't meet Janet outside the door of the study hall, even though she had promised that she would. It was after homeroom and the final dismissal bell when Janet went over to Mirella's locker just as she was closing it.

"Excuse me. I'm sure you didn't mean to forget," Janet said sarcastically, "but could I have my notes back?"

Mirella looked at her lazily. "Sure, just a minute." She thumbed through the books she had with her and then said, "Gee, I'm sorry. I must have locked them in my locker. Mind if I give them to you tomorrow?"

"Sure, no problem," Janet mumbled, wondering again why she lacked the courage to hold Mirella to her promise. She felt so spiritless around Mirella—not just frightened, but weak. Mirella seemed to exude something suffocating, a deadness, like a bad smell, only Janet didn't really smell anything. It was as if the very molecules in the air around her had given up and become her slaves.

Just then, she noticed that Mirella was gazing past her, biting her lower lip. She turned, and sure enough, there was David coming toward them. He was looking straight at Janet, but he must have noticed who she was talking to because he was blushing.

Mirella turned her back on Janet and sashayed up to him. Janet, following close behind, heard her say, "Hi! Isn't this weather outrageous? I sat next to the window in study hall, and that warm breeze almost drove me wild!"

Janet stepped around Mirella and took David's hand. "Sorry I kept you waiting," she said, and walked him away before he had time to speak to Mirella. He smiled at Janet, but she saw the glance he flicked back in Mirella's direction.

Now, as she remembered that quick glance, Janet felt the tears rush to her eyes. That was it— she wanted to cry. She flopped over on her stomach and wept abundantly, burying her face in the pillow to smother her wailing. After a while, her rage eased up. She turned over on her back again and her breathing calmed down. To her surprise, her head felt better. The pain was almost gone.

"I don't care what Mirella is," she said to herself, "but she can't spoil what David and I have. David's head may be turned, but he'll see through her power in the long run."

Suddenly, she felt ravenously hungry. She got up and brushed her hair. It was wonderful just not to have a headache. She smiled at her tear-stained reflection in the mirror and promised it that nobody, certainly not Mirella, was going to ruin her life.

Chapter Three

Cindy didn't care what David and Diane thought about her. Her older brother and sister, like her parents, just didn't seem to understand anything about anything that was important in life. She hoped some of Janet's good sense might rub off on them. Even though Janet was older than Cindy, she always seemed to understand. Even when she didn't fully comprehend, Janet always seemed to believe her. That mattered a lot to Cindy.

Snuggled into her favorite chair, Cindy began to re-read Clayton's journal.

Thursday, April 16, 1907:

Hurrah for spring! Today is one of those crystal days: the sky is a clean, deep blue and the temperature is perfect. The violets are well up on the lawn and the trees are all tingling with the onrush of leaves.

For some reason, I keep putting off the pleasure

of writing about my own happiness. Maybe it's that I hardly dare believe it—I'm reluctant to nail it down with words for fear of killing it. No, I don't mean that! I *must* believe it. See how much I've changed already—maybe my habitual pessimism has received its mortal wound.

Oh, come on, out with it! All right, all right—I'm in love. I love and am loved—ha-ha!!!

Yesterday evening Papa brought the new foreman, George McNulty, and his wife and daughter home for dinner. McNulty seems an unflappable fellow who knows his business and his wife is plump and quiet, with a sort of secret drollness in her attitude. I like her.

And then there was Vera. How can I describe the wonder of seeing her for the first time? I was on the porch and she was getting down from the carriage. It was not like perceiving a stranger— even a beautiful stranger—it was *recognition*. It was like finding someone well known and necessary to me whom I'd forgotten I ever knew—like finishing a jigsaw puzzle—no words can capture the quality of it. When she raised her eyes and met mine, I felt a deep, jarring click, and I knew that she recognized me, too.

While we stood on the porch and waited to be introduced, we looked at each other in sly little winks until finally we were allowed to face each other and take a good deep drink. And then there was that indescribable sense of perfect fitness.

We interlocked without touching. Both of us blushed—that is, she changed color the way one of my peonies does when it opens from a hard white bud into a soft shell-pink bloom, while I merely felt like a freshly scrubbed brick. I think everyone there wanted to burst out laughing, it was so obvious that we were already in love.

It was like that all through dinner. She sat next to Cathy, across from me. We made comical efforts not to look at each other, yet whenever I did steal a peek at her, my glance bounced off hers. And the corners of our mouths constantly struggled not to curl into foolish smiles.

After dinner, we took Vera to see Cathy's studio. She gazed for a while at the little sketch of Papa smoking his pipe, and looked through the whole portfolio of plant and bird watercolors. Cathy and I watched her the whole time; I because I couldn't take my eyes off her, and Cathy because she'd spotted an irresistible subject for a portrait.

After she'd looked at everything, she smiled and said, "It's beautiful." Then Cathy asked Vera if she'd sit for her, and Vera said she'd love to as she darted a glance to me. The color flared in her cheeks again.

She touches my heart so. She's full of life, intelligent, funny, sensitive—her dark eyes sparkle with enjoyment, yet have also the shine of unshed tears. Her hair is so springy that it seems about to burst out of its restraining pins. She will fascinate me forever. Listen to me! It's not even twenty-four hours since we met, yet I know she is my true love.

Cathy invited her to come over tomorrow afternoon and sit for her, after which we'll all take a walk in the woods. She agreed eagerly. She must be used to loneliness, being an only child. She'll never be lonely again if I have anything to say about it.

I'm glad for Cathy's sake, too. They get along like old friends instead of brand new ones. Cathy needs some close female companionship other than Margery's. I think Margery encourages her tendency to mope.

Cindy stretched. She knew she was getting to the good part when Clayton started writing about Margery moping. She also knew that she should go down to dinner, but she just wanted to read this last part again.

She read on:

Actually, Margery is the only fly in the ointment right now. There was a strange moment tonight when we were coming down from the studio and Margery was bringing the children up to bed. We met in the middle of the stairs, and Cathy introduced Vera to Margery and the children. Ralph and Lizzie were very nice and seemed to like Vera, but Margery looked at her with the oddest expression—it was *no* expression really. Her face looked like a mask. I felt Vera immediately become tense. She and Margery glared at each other like—stallions? Ridiculous! But that's what came to mind. We all said goodnight politely and continued on our ways.

I hope Vera's presence in my life will finish

Margery's infatuation with me. It's certainly cleared up the confusion in my own heart. I can admit now that I've felt uncomfortable about Margery ever since the evening Papa brought her home.

Cindy giggled to herself. She knew this part of the story by heart.

"It was a week before Christmas," she said out loud and continued to read:

Papa had been gone all day, bringing Margery from the orphanage in Bridgeport. At last they arrived, and Papa called us to come out and greet her. I was upstairs in my room, writing. I came out and looked over the gallery railing.

Down in the hall, under the chandelier, stood a small but regal figure, cloaked and hooded in a heavy black garment. Snow filled the folds of the cloak. Hidden in the deep hood was a startingly beautiful sphinx-like face, whose beautiful dark eyes looked up and found mine immediately. Holding my gaze with her own, she lifted her long, delicate hands and pushed the hood back, uncovering a mass of very pale, slightly disheveled blond hair.

She looked at me so long and so boldly that it seemed as if she must be trying to purposefully disconcert me. I became offended, and broke the spell—or so I hoped—by saying how-do-you-do as matter-of-factly as possible.

Ever since then, she's made her feelings known to me, quietly but relentlessly. At first I was attracted to her, too. Who would not be moved by such extraordinary beauty? But I've begun to feel that something about her is not what she makes it out to be. She pursues me with such stupid single-mindedness. She has never bothered to get acquainted with me, or to find out what I'm like! There's something unnatural about her.

For the past month or two I've done my best to discourage her. I try to avoid running into her, which is not easy since she has an amazing talent for being in my way. I try especially not to meet her eyes. My behavior is probably almost rude.

She's a capable enough governess for Ralph and Lizzie, I guess. They seem happy, although quieter than they used to be. But I don't like the way she keeps shushing them, quelling their natural rambunctiousness. It wouldn't hurt her to be a little rambunctious herself. She's beautiful, but she's about as much fun as a tub of lard. And she talks so much about her misery at the orphanage, her grief for her unknown parents, etc., etc. It's almost as if she wants to stay unhappy on purpose.

Am I heartless? I'm sure her life has been sad and difficult, but what's the use of making us relive it over and over again? Life is meant to be happy, just as a tree is meant to be green, and so they both will be if they are left alone. Being with Vera for just one evening has made me see that— think what she'll teach me in a lifetime!

Cindy closed the book and smiled. " . . . just as a tree is meant to be green," she thought out loud. Why is it that phrase stuck in her mind every time she read this part of the diary? Could it have something to do with the mystery of Vera and Margery?

"Cindy!" Diane called from the stairs. "Stop playing with those ghosts and come down to dinner!"

Cindy smiled ruefully. Someday her sister would understand . . .

Chapter Four

"Hold on a minute," Janet said to David. "I just have to stop at my locker."

She bent over her lock, but found it hard to focus on the little numbered marks. She and David were on their way to biology lab, their first class of the day, and already the two little discs in her forehead were heavy and beginning to glow red hot.

She took out the books she needed, closed her locker door and said, "I wish we didn't have to start the day with the smell of formaldehyde." Then she turned and saw that she'd spoken to empty air. David had vanished.

Oh no, she thought. Here we go again. She stayed where she was and searched the crowd with her eyes as she fought to control her tears. The past few days it had been much easier for her to start crying than to stop. Finally, she spotted him a little way down the hall, where she knew he would be. He was talking to Mirella as she reclined against her locker door like a goddess against a marble column. Her hair looked like a golden cloud. Her eyes looked with languid smugness into his. Her long white hand drifted like a lazy butterfly to the shoulder of his navy blue sweater and deftly removed something—a curly, reddish-brown hair, no doubt.

Diane appeared beside Janet. "It's just plain weird the way she does that," she said, watching Mirella. "What does she think she is—the Lint Squad?" Then, seeing the look on Janet's face, she added, "She does that to everybody she talks to, you know."

"Oh I *know*," Janet said as her voice wavered out of control. "I *know*. *She* doesn't worry me at all. It's *David* who worries me."

Diane put her arm around Janet's shoulders and gave her a squeeze. Janet could almost hear her friend rummaging through her mind for comforting words. At last she said, "Listen, I know it looks bad, but trust David. I know he hasn't changed his feelings toward you. Really and truly, he's not a flake." The two girls walked down the hall together. "It *is* Mirella who should worry you," Diane continued. "She's one of those people who can't help doing a number on everybody, and she's sure doing one on David."

David and Mirella had stopped ahead of them, near the fire doors. Ronnie Phillips, the star basketball player, came up behind Mirella and put his oversized hand on her shoulder. Mirella leaned back into his hand and pouted at David. Then she turned and walked with Ronnie through the fire doors. David stared after them.

"That does it," Janet muttered as she swallowed and blinked. She was determined not to spill the tears that were burning in her eyes.

"See? She weaves her little spells around everyone," said Diane. "She's getting to be entirely too much. Look, I have to run. Are you okay?"

Janet nodded, not feeling in the least bit okay.

"I'll try to grab Mirella at lunch and have a talk with her," said Diane. "I'll let her know what's what with you and David. Maybe I can straighten things out."

"Oh, would you Diane? That'd be fantastic."

"Sure. Now take it easy. I'll see you later."

The warning bell rang. Through a haze of pain, Janet saw David coming toward her. She walked past him into the lab as if he wasn't there.

It was a miserable morning. When David was around, she didn't speak to him or even look at him. She knew he was watching her. She wasn't trying to punish him; she was simply incapable of turning in his direction.

How could he be doing this to her? Sure, he was her boyfriend and that made it bad enough. But there was even more to it than that. They were connected in a deep, indescribable way. She remembered their conversation in the woods; she wanted to travel through many lives with David. She knew she'd always love him, no matter what.

Yet she was helpless. How could she expect him to resist Mirella? What chance did anyone have against someone with that kind of lethal beauty? Her head hurt so much that for a moment, she considered pleading illness so that she could go home.

Usually, at lunch time David met her and they walked to the cafeteria together. Today, right before lunch, her guts were numb. She wasn't looking forward to confronting him.

As she stood in front of her locker, furiously stuffing books into it, she felt his hands grasp her shoulders. His voice spoke quietly, close to her ear, "Please eat lunch with me."

Slam! went the locker door. She wanted to run away from him. Instead she allowed him to follow her down to the cafeteria, although she neither looked at him nor spoke. As they pushed their trays along beside the steam table, she still did not speak.

She wasn't sure whether or not she was hungry. She gathered a small dish of cottage cheese with a slice of canned pineapple on top of it, a packet of crackers, and a cup of hot water. David, who was behind her, asked for a plate of macaroni and cheese. They paid for their food and stood holding their trays, scanning the noisy room for a place to sit.

With a pang, Janet spotted Mirella and Diane sitting across from each other at an otherwise empty table. They appeared to be deep in talk. Mirella was talking steadily, her hands making a stream of lazy gestures. When Janet felt David lurch involuntarily in their direction, she said firmly, "Let's go over here."

They sat at a different table. Janet refused to look up. She ate her cottage cheese slowly, taking tiny bites. She could tell that David was unhappy—his breathing had a strange rhythm to it. When she had finished eating, she pushed her tray aside, clutched her face between her hands, and massaged her temples with her fingertips.

Huskily, David said, "Jan, please. Why won't you talk to me?"

"I don't know. I just can't find any words." She felt both outraged and trapped. She couldn't see how he could possibly not know why she was upset. On the other hand, she was ashamed to admit that she was jealous. At last the sheer weight of the misery between them forced her to speak.

"How can you not know?" she asked him. "Why do you expect me to do all the talking?"

His eyes had a dull, faraway expression. He wasn't looking straight at her. At last he said, "Are you jealous of Mirella?"

Tremulously, she answered, "Don't I have a reason to be?"

David compressed his lips and stared at his plate. Another silence spread between them while Janet's eyes filled with tears.

David shoved his tray aside, reached across the table for her hand, and held it tight. He looked directly into her eyes for the first time that day. Janet could see the struggle going on within him.

"Can we walk down to the brook after school?" he asked urgently. "I need to talk to you, but we can't really do it now."

"Sure," Janet said, feeling uneasy. "Let's do that. I'll meet you by the flagpole."

Janet did not find a chance during the afternoon to talk to Diane alone. After school, Diane turned up at the flagpole, too, and said she would ride with them as far as the path into the woods. They bicycled up Route 55 to the Sperrys' driveway, where they dismounted. Then they started down the driveway on foot, wheeling their bikes beside them.

Diane walked slowly and thoughtfully, looking at the ground. She seemed to not want to meet Janet's eyes. Janet felt frustrated. She needed to know what had happened at lunch, but couldn't bring it up in front of David. Suddenly, she became aware that David was watching Diane as if he, too, wanted to ask her something—the same question, she realized with a stab of fear.

The silence began to press them uncomfortably hard. At last Diane threw it off. "Well," she began, and the other two held their breaths. "I had quite a talk with Mirella today." After a pause, she continued. "I think I was wrong about her. She's really sweet. She's had an incredibly tough life. She grew up in the slums of Pittsburgh. She doesn't know who her father was. Her mother was a junkie and died of an overdose when Mirella was ten."

"Oh no," said David.

"Yes. So, for the next five years she lived in a foster home with an elderly couple. They were nice but kind of strict, and not very understanding. Six months ago they were both killed in a car accident. So she came to live here with her foster mother's younger sister. The place they live in is kind of shabby, Mirella said. She didn't seem to want to talk about it. She said she's embarrassed to invite people over."

"That's ridiculous. Real friends wouldn't even notice," said David.

"Of course not, but *she'd* mind," said Diane. "And apparently this foster aunt is either always at work or out on a date, or asleep. So Mirella's pretty lonely."

She spoke in a hurried, glib, slightly defensive tone. Watching her, Janet noticed the same evasive, faraway look in her eyes that she'd seen in David's earlier that day. How is it that Mirella could make her two best friends act like zombies?

They came to the place where the wooded path forked away from the driveway and went downhill through the wildlife sanctuary to the brook.

"So I feel kind of different about her," Diane continued, as they stopped walking. "Anyway, I invited her to the party. I hope that's okay," she said, turning to David. "It really made her happy."

"Sure, of course. That's great," said David.

Boiling tears clouded Janet's vision. Abruptly, she turned away, leaned her bicycle against a tree, and ran down the path into the woods. The hot bubble of pain that had been swelling inside her chest all day, pressing up against her larynx, finally burst. She couldn't control her voice any more. It wailed, it roared, it tore her throat. The tears poured down her cheeks.

She knew the path well. After a little distance, it curved to the right around an enormous boulder, then took a steeper plunge downhill. Janet groped her way to the far side of the boulder and leaned against it, letting it hold her up, and surrendered to her weeping. The repeated shock of her heavy sobs lashing through her body touched the pain in her head and seemed to relieve it a little.

She heard the thud of footsteps running down the path, and within seconds David's hands were on her shoulders. She let him turn her around and take her in his arms. He held her tightly until her sobbing had calmed down.

"Di went home so we could be alone," he said. "Come on, let's go down to the brook."

He kept one arm around her as they slowly made their way down the path to the little waterfall where they had sat last summer and talked about reincarnation. Back then, the brook had been only a trickle, creeping under the stones. Now, fattened by the winter's melted snow, it splashed and ran freely. They sat on the big round stones of a crumbled wall. He took her hands and held them.

When she could control her voice, she said, "What's wrong? Everybody's deserting me. First you, now Di—I guess I must deserve it. I'm the only one who doesn't like Mirella. Am I just jealous? I feel like such a horrible person."

"Please don't feel that way, Jan," he said. "There's nothing wrong with you, that's for sure. I do think there's something weird about Mirella, though. I don't know what it is. You may be the only sane person."

"How come you pay attention to her then?"

He rubbed his forehead with one hand. "I don't know. Something comes over me. When she looks at me like that, it's almost hypnotic—it pulls on me. She makes me feel as if I'm the only person in the world who can take care of her and make sense out of her life. She needs me! And part of me hates her and wants to run a mile away, but then something happens and I feel forced to make sure that she's happy."

Anger struck Janet like lightning. Her head throbbed again. "And of course she just happens to be a knockout," she snapped. "I suppose that has nothing to do with it at all." Hearing the sarcasm in her voice, she burst into tears.

David lifted her chin and looked into her eyes. "Lots of people are knockouts," he said as he wiped her tears away with his fingers, "but you're my beautiful you."

Was it just sweet talk? She wanted to believe him. She looked at his eyes and saw that his gaze was steady and tender. She smiled at him. He was back, he was hers again. She could talk to him.

In a rush, she said, "She scares me so much. She is so strange and yet so powerful. She's like some politicians. She smiles and talks sweetly, yet I get the feeling it's just to bully everybody into doing what she wants. I feel as if she could take you away just like *that*"—she snapped her fingers—"without your even noticing." She leaned her forehead against his shoulder. "And now she's coming to the party. What's going to happen? Maybe I shouldn't be there."

"Don't be silly Jan. We couldn't have a party

47

without you," David said. "I need you to be there. I won't let her get to me. I promise." He paused and gently massaged the back of her neck. Suddenly he looked at her and said, "Please be patient with me. It's true—I've got this crazy feeling for her—but I don't want to have it. I don't even like her. It's you I love, absolutely. I don't know what'll happen if you give up on me—except I know I'll be miserable."

Something in his words made her heart sink again. He seemed to keep giving reassurance with one hand and taking it away with the other. But she put her arms around him and held him tightly.

"Of course I won't give up on you," she said. "I'll always be there. I'll stick with you. I just want to be sure you'll stick with me."

When Cindy got home from school that day, she found the house empty. Diane and David weren't home yet; their Mom must be out shopping. She dropped her satchel by the telephone table in the front hall and began to sing loudly, making her voice ring through the empty rooms, as she ran upstairs to change into shorts and a T-shirt. After two glasses of lemonade, she pulled out one of Clayton's old leatherbound notebooks from her satchel, went out to the backyard, and sat down on a low stone. She wanted to swing before she began to read, but something suddenly made her feel very tired and before she realized it, she was fast asleep with the journal tucked between her arms.

When she woke up an hour later, she found herself trembling and muttering, "Please stay, please stay with me and tell me what to do." She looked around and saw the swing and suddenly her dream returned to her in a flash.

In her dream, she had just climbed into the old swing that hung from the maple tree when suddenly she saw someone standing in the yard near the terrace wall where she had left the journal.

"Hey!" she yelled. "That's mine!" The stranger casually looked up, apparently not a bit startled, and began to flip through the book.

Cindy jumped off the swing and landed frog-style on the grass. She stood up and met the eyes of a beautiful, but somehow wild looking, young woman who stood holding the book. Cindy stiffened all over.

"That's my book," she said.

The young woman made no move. When Cindy, forthright as always, stepped up to her and grabbed it away, the young woman didn't even try to hold onto it. She just stood there and smiled.

"You must be Cindy," she said, in a soft, expressionless voice. "I go to school with your brother and sister."

It was Mirella! Cindy thought as she continued to recall her dream.

"What are you doing here?" Cindy remembered asking her. And how did you appear so suddenly? she wanted to ask.

The memory of Mirella made Cindy feel queasy. She was beautiful all right, but too beautiful. How startling was the combination of her very pale blond hair and deep brownish-purple eyes. Her eyes had a shine to them, like that of a cat's in

49

the dark. There was something cat-like in the shape of her eyes, too, and in the lazy way that she blinked. Her whole body had a cat-like grace—solid and sure of itself. Mirella stood there in the yard as if she belonged there as the owner, and Cindy was the stranger.

"I just want to look at your book," she said. Her smile never wavered.

Cindy hugged the book. "I don't think you'd better." Cindy didn't know why she said this, but she felt certain that she wanted to keep that journal out of Mirella's hands.

Mirella took a step toward her and held out her hand. "Please? I won't hurt it. I just need to look at it for a second."

Cindy backed away. Why had this person in her dream made her feel so powerless? Cindy gazed up at the long-lashed, plum-colored eyes, the pearly, velvet-like skin, the way the light looked against the exotic cheekbones, and the creamy rose color in the soft hollows of her cheeks. Why, you can hypnotize yourself just by looking at her, Cindy thought. Then she remembered backing off a few steps, because while she had been standing there entranced, Mirella had come close enough to actually touch the book. She took the corner of it between her thumb and two fingers and gently, as if teasing, tried to pull it out of Cindy's embrace.

It was then that Cindy heard a familiar voice speak a word of warning to her. She jumped and snatched the book out of Mirella's reach. "No! You can't," she said.

She turned her back on Mirella and hurried into the house and up the back stairs. The warning voice whispered, "Quick! Quick!"

"What for?" she asked out loud. "She won't follow me. She'd never find her way up to the tower anyway." But although Cindy remembered that, she still ran quickly to the head of the stairs. Then she stopped to listen. She heard the slow whine of the kitchen door closing and then the click of the latch. Mirella was in the house! Leisurely footsteps crossed the kitchen floor. Why? What was going on? For a moment, Cindy couldn't remember but then, as the footsteps started up the stairs behind her, she remembered flying down the narrow hall through the old servants' quarters when she made a right turn onto the gallery. She panted. It was like a nightmare to be running so hard and getting so tired, while the unhurried footsteps kept gaining, slowly but steadily.

Cindy ran along the gallery and up the stairs to the third floor. At the head of those stairs she stopped again. She heard them again, Mirella's cat-like footsteps, steady as a metronome, tapping across the gallery and along the hall. When she heard them start up the third-floor stairs, she felt a dizzying rush of terror. *How can this be happening? I'm trapped—in my own house!* She looked around wildly. Even now, as she remembered her dream, her vision was blurred by tears of panic.

The next thing Cindy remembered was slamming the door to her bedroom, locking it, and

51

standing right behind it, trying to quiet her breath so she could hear.

The footsteps were still coming. They crossed the hallway and started up the tower stairs. Cindy moved away from the door, her arms folded around the book.

On the top step the footsteps halted. Then came a soft tapping on her door and the low-pitched, toneless voice spoke. "Cindy? I know you're in there. Let me look at your book."

Cindy bit her lip to keep from speaking.

"Cindy? Why are you hiding? You've got nothing to be afraid of. Just show me your book."

The doorknob jiggled. Cindy backed away, her eyes widening. She watched the doorknob shake up and down, up and down, and suddenly, the whole door shuddered and the lock fell to the floor. Cindy gasped. Mirella walked in, still smiling that same smile.

"Won't you let me look at it for a little while? I won't hurt it. Please?" She kept coming toward Cindy, who backed away as she held the book tightly, unable to tear her eyes from the sphinx-like face and glowing eyes.

"How did you get in here?" Cindy screamed. There was a faint smell in the room of something sickening, like rotting meat.

"Really Cindy, why are you making this so difficult? Just let me have the book. It won't hurt. I promise."

"No!" Cindy croaked. She felt as if she was about to choke on her own heartbeat. "No! How did you get in here? I don't want you here. Go away! I want to be alone."

"Give me the book," answered Mirella, "then I'll go."

She continued to come toward Cindy, and Cindy backed into the edge of the open window. She felt the warm air on her back. Every window in this room opened outward, like pairs of glass doors. Cindy was crushed against the west window, the one Margery Smith had fallen out of.

Mirella came closer and closer, and cooed with each step, "Please, Cindy, I'm not going to hurt you. Please angel, I'm not going to hurt you as long as you let me read your book." Mirella's hand touched the book, her fingers curling over the edge. Cindy tried to pull it away, but there was nothing behind for her to brace herself against except the breeze. Suddenly, she realized that Mirella was no longer trying to take the book, but instead was pushing Cindy. Her knuckles dug deeply into her chest and Cindy gasped with pain. She felt the empty height behind her, reaching for her. Nausea filled her throat. She shut her eyes tightly and tried to scream, but nothing came out except for a tiny, high-pitched whimper, like a puppy being strangled. Cindy wrestled but she couldn't get free from the stony knuckles that drove into her chest. They were too strong. It was over, she was falling—

Just as her feet were about to lose the floor, she woke up. The pressure of those knuckles vanished. But a vague feeling of firmness around her shoulders remained. The voice that had warned her before whispered, "It's over. You're safe."

Had she only imagined Mirella gasping and grunting? Or did it really happen? Cindy blinked. She couldn't be sure.

She opened her eyes. Mirella was gone. No one was there. She sat upright, breathing deeply. She felt a vague pain in her chest. What a weird dream, she thought.

Clutching her book, Cindy walked over to the swing. "Please save me," she whispered. "Whoever you are, please save me."

Chapter Five

At supper that night Cindy turned to her father and said, "Dad, do you have any plants that might do well up in the tower? I'd like some in my room."

"Why sure," he said. "That's a great idea. There are lots of things that would love it up there. After supper let's go out to the conservatory and take a look."

"And I was thinking," Cindy continued, "would it be okay if I started some cuttings in those empty rooms on the third floor?"

"Why not?" answered her mother.

Diane raised her eyebrows and David opened his mouth to speak, but a swift glance from their mother prevented him. Cindy said no more. She knew her family was silently cheering her interest in plants as a hobby that might be traded for her fascination with ghosts.

Just as well, she thought.

Later that evening, a young avocado tree and

three spider plants were carried to Cindy's bedroom. One morning a few days later, Mrs. Sperry discovered rows of newly transplanted little spider plants and philodendra on the windowsills of every room on the third floor. In the closets and dark areas, slips of ivy and begonia stood in water-filled jars, already growing roots.

Cindy wasn't sure the plants would work, but after reading more in Clayton's diary, she had had a hunch. His journal entry of May 8, 1907 began this way:

Life seems too beautiful to bear! Vera doesn't like me to say that. She says life doesn't just seem beautiful, it *is* beautiful, and the things we call "too good to be true" are the very things that are true.

We took a walk today which began beautifully but ended very strangely. At first, only Vera and Cathy and I were going to go. However, just as we were leaving, Margery appeared right by the porch steps with Ralph and Lizzie, so we had to invite them along.

What a strange person Margery is! As we set off, I got the feeling that she was of two minds about going. One mind wanted to keep an eye on Vera and me. The other mind really doesn't like the woods at all. It was so queer. Although the air was delightfully warm, she wore a shawl tightly around her as if she was afraid of a draft. I don't think she likes the woods at all because as we entered them, she drew up her skirts and walked carefully in the center of the path as if she was afraid she would brush against plants in a poisonous jungle.

The woods were bursting with growth. You could feel the energy surge up from the ground. We saw tiny leaves with little blaze-like green flames. It is as if the twigs they grow from are the wicks and the earth holds the fuel they burn.

Ralph and Lizzie dashed off the path and ran around wildly, trampling things and pulling them up by the roots. I've never seen them so unrestrained. Usually they remember what I've taught them about walking in the woods, but today they were like animals themselves, set free after having been cooped up too long. Margery kept calling to them to stop, to come back, to behave, but I told her to leave them alone. I could plainly see the pent-up anger in their noisiness and I thought they should be allowed to run it off. Like true love, the woods will survive. Nothing can kill that kind of life.

Vera and I tried to drift away from the others. When we go out for a walk with Cathy alone, it works out well—Cathy is tactful enough to stop now and then and look through her field glasses so that we can steal a kiss. But today, Margery was glued to Cathy's elbow and she was forever looking back at us over her shoulder. Then she'd go on lecturing Cathy, which she does incessantly. About what, I have no idea. Cathy didn't resist, but walked along quietly, her head down.

Vera was annoyed with Cathy for putting up with Margery. "Whenever Margery gets hold of her like that, she gives up," she said. "Look at her—she almost looks as scared of the woods as Margery does!" Then she added, "It's odd, really. Margery thinks she's crazy about you, yet she obviously hates the woods. How could anybody even imagine loving you and not expect to spend most of her time covered with burrs, or tangled in brambles, or ankle-deep in muck, pulling watercress out of icy streams? Not Margery's idea of fun, from the looks of things!"

How I longed to seize her and wrap us both up in brambles, so that we could never be separated. But before I could, we heard Ralph yelling, "Clay! Clay! What's this?"

We looked up and saw him running toward us, waving a clump of uprooted plants. As he pushed past Cathy and Margery, there was the most awful, ear-splitting shriek. Ralph stopped in his tracks. Vera and I ran up to them.

Margery was standing like a statue, her hands covering her face. Cathy asked her what was wrong. "Nothing!" she replied but when she took her hands away, we saw that her face was deadly pale, almost blue. She insisted again that she was all right, but she swayed slightly and I could hear her breath wheezing in her throat. When Ralph came up to her, still holding the plants, she shrank into Cathy's arms, screaming, "Get rid of that stuff! What if it's poison?"

I examined the plants, but they were only vervain. I threw them away. We were all astonished—we'd never seen Margery get in the least flustered before, and here she was practically hysterical. She complained of a cramp in her foot, so we started home. At Margery's insistence, Vera and I helped her along, one on each side, while Cathy took charge of the children. Margery moaned a good deal, and leaned her head first on Vera's shoulder, then on mine. Odd behavior to go with a cramp in the foot, I thought.

When we got back to the house, Cathy took Margery and the children indoors. Vera and I hitched up Maxie and I drove her home. She was silent and looked pale and tired. She admitted that something was bothering her, but said she didn't know how to put it into words. On the porch, she gave me a strange smile. It was sad, knowing, a little sardonic. For a moment, I felt as if she was drifting out of my reach. I pulled her to me and held her tight.

I must ask her to marry me soon.

Chapter Six

"Now then!" said Janet, lunging like a karate master toward her reflection in the full-length mirror on her closet door. She wore her white terry cloth bathrobe and a pink towel was wrapped around her wet hair. "Here we go! Look out, world!"

It was time to get ready for the Sperrys' party. She had been psyching herself up for it all day. She was determined to be at her best, to stay on top of the situation and have a good time. Neither Mirella nor any old headache was going to spoil her fun.

She'd come home from school with a headache every single day this past week. So far today, Saturday, she felt pretty good. In the middle of the afternoon she had begun to be aware of those two discs but she had taken some aspirin and gone to sleep for a couple of hours. After she woke up, she tried not to think about her head. Her mother said you could make yourself sick just by watching too hard for symptoms, and Janet thought she was right.

"Ohhh-kay! Onward and upward!" she went on. "What shall I wear?" She put on her underwear, opened her closet door, and stood there, considering.

She knew most people would be wearing jeans, but she felt like dressing up. "Why not?" she said out loud, as she pulled out a long, V-neck caftan. Its crimson color brought out something exotic in her, setting off her long dark hair and the flash in her eyes. For a moment she hesitated, thinking of the contrast she would make with the rest of the crowd, but then she decided that would be just fine. Tonight was a night to stand out.

"Oooh boy! You're wearing that?" Amy appeared in the doorway. "Is anybody in here? I heard you talking to somebody."

"Nope—I was just talking to myself."

Amy climbed on the bed and asked, "Can I fix your hair? I'll curl it for you."

"Sure, why not?" said Janet. "Go to it." She handed her sister a comb and the blow-dryer and sat down at her dressing table. She leaned back so that her heavy, wet mop of hair hung over the back of the chair.

Amy first combed the tangles out of Janet's hair, then took the dryer and went to work. Janet relaxed and closed her eyes. How pleasant it was to be fussed over . . . but just then, a pain struck like a match behind her eyes. Her heart sank. That fiery throb was a familiar warning—a signal that within a few hours her skull would feel like a cauldron of molten lead.

"Rats," she said, before she could stop herself.

"What's wrong?"

"Oh, nothing, just my head," she said. "It's been fine all day, but it just now acted up. The last thing I want is to have a headache at this party."

Amy said, "You know what I think? I think you spend too much time at the Sperrys'."

Janet was astonished. "Too much time at the Sperrys'! They're my friends! *Our* friends! Why shouldn't I spend as much time there as I want? You're always over there yourself, playing with Cindy—" She stopped, realizing that Amy hadn't been there lately. "Or you used to be," she corrected herself, beginning to sense what was bothering Amy. "What's going on with you and Cindy?"

"It's the ghosts," said Amy. "She doesn't talk about them any more, but she's gotten really weird. She won't play with me, because she says I don't understand her. She says the ghosts are her only friends." Amy's voice shook a little. "I'm scared. What if they've *got* her—you know, in their power—what if they're driving her crazy? A lot of people think the Dexters were murderers. What if it's the ghosts giving you these headaches? I wish you wouldn't go there so much!"

Janet could see Amy's lower lip trembling and her eyes filling up with tears.

"Never mind that," she said as she turned to face her sister. She took her hands. "Now listen, Amy, don't worry. Two things to remember. First, I don't think there are any ghosts in that house, but even if there were, ghosts are sometimes good spirits . . ."

"Janet! You don't believe in them do you?" Amy's voice shook.

"I'm not saying that I believe there are ghosts in the Sperry house right now, but I do believe that a soul can come back to life in a different form than the one it first used. I suppose you could call that a ghost."

Amy's shoulders drooped.

"And second thing, Amy," continued Janet, "don't worry about my headaches." She squeezed Amy's hands, then turned back to the mirror and began to put on her make-up. "If anybody's giving me a headache, it's a real live person—and not anybody who lives or ever did live at the Sperrys'!"

"Who?" Amy asked.

"That new girl, Mirella. She likes David entirely too much, and it's getting to me. David was sort of taken in at first, but now he sees through her, I think. Anyway, she's coming to this party, so it's no time for me to have a headache."

"Just do what Mom says," said Amy. "Know that you have the power to make the headache go away, and keep telling yourself you feel fine."

"I'm working on it, I'm working on it!" muttered Janet.

"You do look a little pale," said Amy.

"I do not!" exploded Janet. But she could see it herself. Her forehead twanged with fire again. Was she really going to have to fight off the headache all evening?

"You don't have to get mad—just put on some blush," said Amy.

"You're right," said Janet. She applied the color to her cheeks, then stood up and slipped into the caftan.

Sandals and a midnight blue shawl completed the ensemble. Surveying the full effect in the mirror, she thought she'd never looked better. The vibrant crimson and deep blue made her eyes snap.

Amy exclaimed, "Ooh—you look super!" and insisted on fixing her hair once more.

Janet stood up in the Sperrys' front hall before any other guests had arrived. The old house had been transformed. The doors and windows were open to the warm, fragrant spring night. The rooms were decorated with candles and bowls of fresh flowers. In the hall the rugs had been taken up and the wood floor polished.

Looking around, Janet imagined that she could hear the whispers of voices from another time. It was strange to think that the hall would soon be filled with people in blue jeans dancing to music booming from the stereo, instead of white-gloved couples waltzing while a little orchestra played in the gallery above.

"You know," she said to Diane as the two of them arranged plates of food on the dining room table. "The house feels old-fashioned tonight. The candlelight brings it out. Wouldn't it be neat if the Dexters were having their own invisible party at the same time ours was going on!"

Cindy, who was there in her pajamas and bathrobe, raised her eyebrows at Janet and winked in her direction as she went back into the kitchen. Before Janet could think about the look, Diane flashed her friend a look as if to say, "You're starting to sound like my crazy kid sister, old buddy." Janet shrugged. She didn't want to cause a problem, but she couldn't deny her own senses, either. There was definitely something unusual in the air, a crackling that she could almost hear, like the rustling of long skirts and tapping of satin shoes. This same soft, sparkling light had filled these rooms seventy-five years ago. The fragrance of these flowers—or flowers born of Clayton's flowers—mingled with the spring night air. Why not just let go and pretend—but pretending wasn't the right word. It would be more like *not* pretending. What would happen if she gave in, opened her inner ears to those almost-heard whispers, and said, "Yes, I know you're here!"

"Hey, Cindy!" she called. "Why don't you show me the plants I'm supposed to water while you're away?"

Cindy brought a big bowl of potato chips out of the kitchen and set it down next to the sour cream dip. "Sure," she said.

"Light the candles in the conservatory while you're out there, would you?" asked Diane, tossing Janet a box of miniature wooden matches.

Janet and Cindy left the dining room through its tall glass double doors. To their left as they faced the front door was the great staircase. Opposite the staircase, on their right, was the door to the living room. Janet was just about to follow Cindy into the living room when out of the corner of her eye, she caught a flash of pink moving along the gallery.

Quickly she looked up over her right shoulder. No one was there. But the instant replay of her memory kept repeating the flash: a beautiful girl in a long pink dress, moving swiftly along the gallery toward the head of the stairs. She could swear she'd seen her. A strange chill ran through her. And then she heard, as if right inside her ear, the clear cascade of a woman's laughter.

She whipped around. It had not been Diane or Cindy. Could it have been someone outside, just arriving? No, the hall was empty.

Cindy noticed the odd expression on her face, but said nothing. She showed Janet the few plants in the living room that would need watering, then led the way into the conservatory.

In the old days, when it had been Clayton Dexter's favorite room, there were not only a great many plants, but also a roll-top desk, a chair, and a small bookshelf. Mike Sperry, an avid gardener, had filled the room with plants again, and had put in a desk and chair much like Clayton's. The air was moist, earthy, and delicious from the oxygen released by the leaves.

For the party, the twins had set white candles all around the plants. Janet stopped before each candle, struck a match, and offered the pale wick a sip of flame. A transparent yellow bud grew from the point of contact. As she blew out the match, she looked up and saw her own candlelit face reflected in the night-blackened window. It didn't quite look like her own: the eyes were unusually

66

wide and dark, as if she were startled or on the alert. Then, in her mind she again saw the woman in pink and heard her laugh. Each candle she lit gave her another reflection of herself to look at, and with it another replay of the vision and the laughter.

Somebody wants to speak to me, she heard herself think.

When all the candles were lit, Cindy said, "I've got some plants upstairs. Do you think you could water them, too, when you come?"

"Sure," said Janet. "Why don't you show them to me now?"

The girls left the conservatory and climbed up to the third floor. First, Cindy showed her the cuttings and young transplants she had on the windowsills. "There's a plastic jug under the sink in the bathroom over there," she said, waving her hand. "Just fill it, and make sure these aren't dried out." Janet found it odd that Cindy had scattered her plants about that way, a few in each room, instead of keeping them all in the sunny tower, but she didn't say anything.

As they climbed the short winding staircase that led from the third floor up to the tower, Cindy rushed ahead of Janet into her room, and hastily hid something under the pillow.

Janet stood in the doorway. "Wow, you're really into plants!" she said, admiring the potted avocado tree beside the west window and the spider plants hanging in front of the others. "You could have a greenhouse like your Dad's up here, couldn't you?"

"I like plants. They're special to me," Cindy replied.

"Yes, I know what you mean," said Janet. "I mean, to think that in a way, they never die. They just live on forever. A never-ending vital force. It's amazing."

Cindy assessed her friend's older sister. Was it possible that Janet understood?

"I miss Amy," she said.

"Well, you know," said Janet. "Amy feels really hurt that you don't play with her any more. What's wrong?"

Cindy sat down on the edge of the bed and folded her arms tightly. "Nothing," she said.

"Look," Janet persisted. "Amy is your friend and she misses you, too. Don't you care how she feels? She says you're so wrapped up in your ghosts that—"

"Ha!" said Cindy. "That's what's wrong, if you really want to know. Nobody believes anything I say, so what's the use of talking to anybody? What's the use of having friends, or brothers and sisters, or parents, if they just treat you like a nut when you tell them the truth?" She spoke indignantly, with irony and pain.

Janet was stymied for a moment. Then she said, "Okay, Cindy. I'm sorry. I believe you, you know I do. I just don't like seeing Amy hurt, that's all."

"Promise you won't tell anybody—not the twins, not my parents, not *anybody*? I'm sick of being laughed at."

"I promise."

"Just tell Amy that I like her fine, and I miss

68

her, too, but I can't play with her right now."

"Okay."

Cindy leaned forward and gazed into Janet's eyes. She looked so wise and serious that for a moment, Janet wanted to laugh. She didn't, but Cindy saw the tug at the corner of her mouth and she cried, "You better not laugh! Or I won't tell you anything!"

"I won't, I promise."

"Okay, then. Look—the ghosts are real, I swear they are. And they're *good*. Mrs. Wiggins at the library used to know Cathy very well. She says Clay and Cathy were very gentle people, kind and funny. They'd never hurt anyone."

"How do you know their ghosts are here?"

"I can feel them. When I go into a room and one of them is there, or if they come into a room where I am, I can feel a sort of, a sort of a—" Cindy closed her eyes and waved her hands, looking for a way to say it. "A sort of very strong, *important funniness* in the air, like when someone keeps trying to tell you a joke—only it's more than that, it's the feeling of *one certain person and no other*—do you know what I mean?"

"Yes," said Janet slowly, "I think I do."

"People think all ghosts are bad," said Cindy disgustedly. "They think that just because you're a ghost, you're compelled to be mean, but it's not true. What kind of ghost you are depends on what kind of person you are. Or were. So if a ghost wants to let a live person know he's there, he won't do it in a mean way unless he was a mean person when he was alive."

"I see," said Janet, fascinated.

"You have to use your common sense around ghosts. You have to relax and let yourself feel what they're like. Then you know if they're bad or not. The feeling is the most important sign a ghost can give you." Cindy narrowed her eyes. "They give other kinds of signs, too. Like the first time I ever got the feeling Cathy was around."

"What happened?"

"It was when we first moved in here, and I'd just finished fixing up this room. I took the hammer back down to the basement, and when I came back up here, all the curtains started dancing around, as if the wind was blowing them—but the windows were all closed! They went on dancing for about ten minutes, and during that time I kept noticing this really strong feeling of *somebody* in the room. And I just knew it was Cathy. I think she made the curtains dance in order to make me notice her and identify the feeling. This was her room, you know."

"I know." Sounds of the party getting under way began to reach them from two floors below. Janet suddenly saw the woman in pink again, her dark hair piled on top of her head in a Gibson girl style. She was standing on the gallery looking down at the crowd in the hall. Janet turned to Cindy and asked, "Do you ever *see* them?"

For an instant, Cindy's expression contracted, as if an unpleasant memory were crossing her mind. Then she recollected herself and said, "Only in my dreams. Sometimes they come and tell me where to find things I've lost. I know it's them because the feeling is so strong, and they're somehow extra definite, much more real than people in dreams usually are."

"What do they look like?"

"Well, Clay is tall and has sandy-colored hair, a mustache and blue eyes. Cathy has the same color hair and wears it piled on top of her head. They both have narrow faces, and a way of crinkling their eyes that makes them look happy and sad at the same time. Usually they wear brown and dark green—woodsy colors."

"You feel them in the daytime, as well as at night?"

"Oh sure. Any time. They don't only appear in the dark."

"Hmmm," said Janet. "Well—are they in the room right now?"

Cindy closed her eyes and held herself still, as if she were listening for a faraway signal. When she opened her eyes, they were wider and darker than usual.

"Just a little. I mean, only very faintly. It's hard to explain. Now that they're free of their bodies, they don't have to stay pinpointed to any one place. They can spread themselves out through the whole house if they want. Right now they're mostly downstairs—I think they want to be near the party. But there's a little of them up here, too. Wait—" she closed her eyes again.

Just then, Diane called up to them from the third-floor landing, "Hey, Jan! There's a party going on!"

Cindy put her hand on Janet's arm to hold her

back. Janet called, "I'll be right down!"

Cindy opened her eyes and looked at Janet piercingly. "I'm getting something," she whispered. The vibrations from the disco music began to vibrate through the house, but she didn't seem to notice. "They want me to tell you something. They want you to be careful! I think they're saying that you're in some kind of danger!"

"Oh great," said Janet, keeping her voice on the casual side of seriousness. "From what?" Cindy's words had sent a shiver through her. She thought it was time to break the mood, but she wanted to do it gently.

"I don't know. But I'm getting the feeling, and it's really strong. How's your headache?"

Janet was surprised that Cindy knew to ask about it. She gave her head a shake and said, "It feels okay."

"Good," said Cindy. She got into bed and continued. "Look Jan, please believe me—and be careful!"

Janet stood up and looked down at her. "I'll be careful," she said. "Want me to turn out your light?"

"No thanks. I'm going to read for a while."

In the gallery, Janet paused to look down into the hall. The party was in full swing. Disco music blared. Janet scanned the crowd for David but he was nowhere in sight. Suddenly, she spotted him coming out of the living room with Diane and

Mirella. The three of them worked their way around the edge of the hall and headed for the stairs.

Mirella was wearing designer jeans and a dark blue Indian blouse with a scoop neck. A little red satin bag, fastened to her belt, hung against her hip. The outfit accentuated the voluptuous perfection of her body. Her hair was a shimmering mane. People in the hall stole glances at her as she climbed the stairs. She seemed to be radiating her sexiness in all directions, not focusing it on David, and he looked numb, as if he was trying to conceal how enraptured he was.

Despair knocked hard on Janet's heart and her head throbbed. As they came up the stairs, she braced herself. But David took her hand firmly and said, "Oh, there you are!" She melted and went with them.

Mirella led them, as if she knew her way around. She glanced into each of the bedrooms that opened off of the hallway—as though she was just checking it out. When they came to the stairs that led up to the third floor, she stopped as if ready to go back. But Diane said, "Oh, you have to see the third floor! If Cindy's still awake, she'll let us show you the tower."

Mirella hesitated. Just then, there was a sound of scurrying feet above them and a door slammed. Mirella started and turned pale. It was the first time Janet had seen her even slightly unnerved.

"What's wrong, Mirella?" she asked. "That was just Cindy, running back to bed. She must have been spying on the party. Don't you want to see the tower? It's really incredible." She felt a reckless impulse to toy with Mirella.

But Mirella was not to be pushed around. "No thanks! I don't want to go up there—it's not my kind of place," she said, letting a tiny glance at David escape from under her long lashes. "Let's go back to the party."

Back downstairs, Mirella and Diane joined the crowd on the dance floor.

"What's going on?" asked David. They went through the living room to the hall. It was so crowded with people that at first they couldn't see what was going on. Everyone was packed into a ring, leaving a space in the middle of the floor. Then they saw it.

Mirella was dancing a solo. Slowly, sinuously, rippling and quivering, she twisted her limbs around in the air, possessing it. There were more wolf whistles. She silenced them with a flash of her eyes and then began to move faster, more wildly, stamping her feet as if to impress her own heavy rhythm into the shapeless swamp of the music. She whirled and undulated, shaking her pale blond mane. Her enormous dark eyes glowed, her nostrils flared, and her raspberry mouth was wide open. She flung her body into shapes which, on anyone else, would have been mere contortions. On her, they were ciphers that were full of hidden meanings.

It was as if she were presenting them with a message, a warning, Janet felt. A declaration of ancient power, dark and irresistible.

Everyone watched, entranced. No one clapped

or whistled any more, or even whispered.

"This is unreal," Janet said to David in a low voice.

"Outrageous," said Diane, on the other side of him. "She's not even sweating."

David didn't say anything. He couldn't. He was watching Mirella as if he was mesmerized. Janet squeezed his elbow gently but he didn't seem to feel it.

"Hey! Are you there?" she asked. "Don't forget what you promised—"

He smiled absently and touched her cheek. "Oh, don't worry. I won't," he said, tonelessly.

Tears stung Janet's eyes. Her head began to throb and burn.

The music faded out in a discordant snarl of trumpets and saxophones. Mirella ended her dance and stood with her feet apart and her arms stretched above her head, fists clenched. Her expression blazed with ferocity. Then she dropped the pose, lowered her arms and smiled. Somehow, Mirella seemed taller now, a more formidable presence, even more so than usual. There was some applause, which she barely acknowledged with a nod. Then she spoke—a celebrity being chummy with her audience.

"Thanks, everybody! And now, I want to ask all of you a favor." She opened her red satin bag and took out a felt-tip pen, a roll of masking tape, and a pair of embroidery scissors. She held the scissors up, opening and closing them so that the gleaming blades flashed, and said loudly, "Before I leave tonight, I want every single person here to give me a lock of hair. For a souvenir."

Janet felt a heavy shock echo through her body. She turned to speak to David but he was gone. She couldn't see him anywhere. Mirella was in the center of a cluster of people, all waiting for her to cut their hair.

Feeling sick, lonely, and afraid, Janet wandered into the dining room and collected a stack of dirty paper plates, which she then took out to the kitchen to dump into the garbage pail. Her hands were trembling. When she got back to the hall, she saw Annie Lombardo go up to Mirella and bend her dark curly head. Mirella snipped a lock from the nape of Annie's neck and wrapped it in a piece of the masking tape, and then wrote something down—Annie's initials? She dropped the sample into her little red bag. Next, Lenny Johnson came up to her, eager for his turn. And after Lenny, Carol Ascher, and after Carol, Jeanie Scanlon. Everyone seemed willing to have their hair shorn.

Janet leaned against the doorway. Her head throbbed and her legs were weak. Suddenly, she realized her fear was turning into terror. She tried to tell herself that she was being unreasonable. Surely Mirella wasn't doing any harm—but when Janet saw Diane smile and bend her head to the scissors, she almost screamed out, "Diane—don't!" But before she could open her mouth, the scissors flashed. The reddish-brown curl was rolled in tape, labelled, and stuffed into the bag.

By now Mirella had collected hair from everyone except Janet, David, and Tommy Jones. Tommy's hair was shaved close to his scalp except for a little punk rock style pigtail in the back. He was proud of that pigtail and didn't want to lose any part of it, but Mirella wouldn't leave him alone. She followed him from room to room until at last, he gave in. There was scattered applause as the scissors robbed him of a curl. He watched with a bewildered, mournful expression as his single braided curl disappeared into the red satin bag.

Janet spotted David leaning against the post at the foot of the stairs. She hurried up to him and put her hands on his arm.

"David," she said urgently, "don't let her cut your hair!"

He looked at her, or *almost* at her. But Janet knew he didn't see her. "What's wrong, Jan?" he asked. "What's the harm? Everybody else did it."

"I know—I don't know—" She felt idiotic. "I just hate it, that's all."

"Jan, where's your sense of humor? It's just a joke. It doesn't mean anything."

Her eyes filled with tears. "But it's so—*gruesome!*" she said, with a sob. "Oh David, please— for me, for my sake, even if you do think I'm crazy—"

People were staring.

David took her by the shoulders. "Now calm down," he said in a low voice. "Get hold of yourself, Janet. Is your head hurting again? Want to go upstairs and lie down for a while?"

Just then, Mirella came in from the dining room. "Oh, there you are!" she called. "Last, but not least!"

Smiling that wicked little smile, she came up to Janet and sneered in her face. Up close, her smoky plum-colored eyes appeared shallow, reflecting the light in a strange way as if they had foil inside of them. "Why Janet, what's wrong?" she purred, mockingly. "There's nothing to be afraid of."

A searing pain shot through Janet's head.

"She's just being silly," said David. He stood beside Mirella as if the two of them were ganging up on her. "Just watch," he said to Janet as he bowed his head. Mirella's long white fingers sank into the glossy red-brown curls. The scissors flashed. "See? Nothing to it," he said, straightening up.

"Ready?" smiled Mirella, reaching out for Janet's dark mass of hair.

Janet recoiled. She didn't know why, but she wouldn't let Mirella cut her hair. She knew she just couldn't. Gathering all of her hair into her left hand, she backed away and stepped onto the wide lower landing of the staircase. Mirella followed her.

"Aw Jan, come on. There's nothing to be afraid of," she said.

Panic and revulsion hit Janet like a heavy fist in her stomach. Screaming "NO! NO!" she turned and fled up the stairs. Mirella followed close behind.

In the hall, everyone stopped to watch the chase. "Go, Mirella!" someone yelled.

Why is everyone against me? thought Janet. She was just able to keep ahead of Mirella's reach.

She could feel the incredible power of Mirella's determination to catch her, and knew that she must not be cornered.

The third floor—Mirella hadn't wanted to go up there before! With sudden hope, Janet sprinted up the stairs. She heard the cruel tapping of Mirella's high-heeled sandals on the wooden steps behind her. Without realizing the words were out of her mouth, Janet began to yell wildly, "Cindy! Cindy!" and ran straight across the third-floor hall toward Cindy's room.

Light suddenly splashed down the little spiral staircase as Cindy opened her door. "Up here, Janet!" called a small pajama-clad figure silhouetted against the brightness. Janet scrambled up the stairs and stood beside her. The sound of pursuing footsteps had stopped. Mirella had climbed only partway up the third-floor stairs.

"Relax, Janet. I don't need your hair that badly," they heard her call. Then the footsteps went back down and faded away.

Janet was gasping for breath. She followed Cindy into her room and sat down on the bed. "She wants to cut a piece of my hair off," she told Cindy. "She's taken a sample from everyone who's here. Except mine. I don't know why, but it freaks me out."

Cindy looked at her gravely and nodded. "Just wait here until she's gone," she said. "She can't come up here because of the plants."

"Because of the *plants*?" Janet wasn't sure she'd heard right. But something in Cindy's face stopped her from pressing for an explanation.

David appeared in Cindy's doorway looking flushed and anxious. "Here you are!" he said to Janet. "You had me worried, running away like that. What's the matter? Why are you acting so weird?" He came and stood in front of her and took her face in his hands.

"I'm sorry," she said. "I guess I am weird. I just don't want her to cut my hair, that's all." Janet was almost whispering.

"Well, don't worry. She won't. She says she's given up. Please come back down."

"I'll come, too," said Cindy. "I can't sleep anyway."

"Oh no you won't," David told her. "It's way too late for you. Mom would kill me if I let you."

Cindy didn't say anything.

Janet's head ached. She felt trapped, defeated. "Okay, I'll come," she said. She followed David out of the room. At the door, she turned. "Thanks a million, Cindy."

"Not at all," said Cindy as she winked at her.

The party was in its final phase. A few people were still dancing and the rest had gathered into small groups, finishing up the beer. Many were playfully wrestling over bits of each other's clothing or jewelry, trying to steal them for souvenirs. Mirella's hair collecting had started a fad.

Mirella herself was nowhere to be found, but Janet felt shaky and suspicious. She stood close to David, furtively checking the different groups of people for the one person she dreaded seeing. But the light was so dim and the traffic so heavy that there was no certainty about who was where.

"Want a beer?" David asked her. She nodded. "Wait here. I think there are a few left." He vanished in the direction of the dining room.

I don't want a beer, Janet thought. I want to go to sleep. But I must not let my eyes close. I don't dare. Someone might sneak up on me. Her head fell forward anyway. Where's David? He's been gone so long. My eyes are so heavy. Maybe I'll let them close, just for a minute . . .

Is something touching my hair? Yes. YES!

It was that horrible, obscenely gentle touch. Janet jerked her head around and at the same moment heard an explosive crash, followed by a blood-curdling scream.

A terra cotta pot lay smashed on the floor in the hall. Shards, earth, and broken fern fronds still skated in all directions. Janet's wrist was seized by a small, strong hand. She looked down and there was Cindy, staring with blazing eyes across the hall. Janet followed the direction of her gaze and saw Mirella clinging to the newel post as if she had been blown there by the crash. It was Mirella who had screamed.

She was deadly pale, almost blue, and looked as if she was asphyxiating. Her lips, the color of clay, were drawn back from her teeth. Her face, full of loathing, glared down at the plant and then across at Cindy. Cindy met her stare without flinching.

"She was just about to cut your hair," she told

Janet. "But I was hiding over there," she pointed across the doorway, "and I threw the plant at her. I knew it would scare her away."

Janet was speechless. Why the plant? She could have thrown anything—a shoe would have done the job. But why the *plant*?

Mirella's eyes narrowed and a laser of hate shot out of them. Her lips twitched as if to sneer, but then they resumed their habitual smile. The color returned to her face. She shrugged her shoulders, gave a debonair little wave, and walked out through the front door.

Everyone stood there, stunned. David began to clean up the mess. The fern lay on the floor like a fish out of water. Cindy gathered it up tenderly. "I'll repot it," she said. "I know it'll be okay. Plants always come back to life."

Janet followed her to the conservatory. The soft, moist air was a relief after the smoky atmosphere of the other rooms, but Janet was in such pain that she could hardly tell where she was any more—she only knew that she was not home in bed. She sat down on top of a short wooden stepladder, and watched dully as Cindy found an empty pot and replanted the fern.

David came in. "Cindy, what exactly is going on?" Then he saw Janet and he put his arms around her. "Janet, what is it? Are you okay? What's wrong with everybody? I don't understand."

Janet couldn't stop trembling. She held her head in her hands. "I'm a mess," she said. "My head hurts so much I can't see straight. I have to go home."

She was only dimly aware of David carrying her out to the car, and even less aware of the ride home. By the time he pulled up in front of her house, she was just barely able to open her eyes.

"I had no idea how sick you were," he said.

"I have to ask you something," she said. "Why did you and Mirella gang up on me?"

He frowned. "Gang up on you?"

"About my hair. I was really upset. I didn't want her to cut it, and when you urged me to let her do it, it freaked me out."

He looked at her, obviously troubled. "I don't know what you mean," he said. "I'd never gang up on you. What are you talking about? Nobody was ganging up on you—I swear."

"Remember? The hair and Mirella's nasty little scissors. Remember?"

"Janet, I don't think you're feeling too well. Maybe we should talk about this in the morning."

"David! Two hours ago, you had more hair on your head than you do now!"

"Right, Janet," he answered. She knew he didn't believe her, but it didn't matter right now. Nothing did, except for the throbbing pain in her head.

"You're sick, that's what it is," David said. He put his arms around her. "You should see a doctor."

"I don't like doctors, and anyway, I think this is exactly the kind of thing they don't know how to treat."

"Don't talk nonsense, Janet. I just don't want you to take any chances. Please." He kissed her. "You know what you mean to me."

As Janet turned to enter her house, she thought: do I?

Chapter Seven

That night Cindy spent hours reading by the dull glow of her night light. She felt certain that if she only read deep enough into Clayton's journals, she would understand. She turned to the page marked May 14, 1907:

The house and countryside are a giant musical instrument being played upon by trillions of tireless watery fingers. It's almost as damp indoors as out.

Mama is still away at Grandmother's. Papa is at the ironworks until late every evening. The spirits of those left behind, trapped in all this gray-green gloom, are melancholy and impatient. I love the rain, ordinarily, but I miss Vera so. She's been ill, and I haven't seen her for almost a week. As soon as I see her I'm going to ask her to marry me.

I can't wait! I think I'll do it very offhandedly, as if I were asking her to pass the sugar. She'll answer in the same tone: "Why yes, that might be rather nice." And then we'll laugh.

In a way it's just as well that she can't visit us right now. The mood here is so low. Cathy, in particular, is not herself. She has little energy and no sense of humor. Most of the time she's in her room, alone or with Margery, and when she comes out it's obvious that she's been crying. She hardly speaks to me—she seems to need all her strength just to hold back the tears. I'm really worried about her. I try to talk to her, but she only weeps and scolds.

I wish I knew exactly what Margery says to her in those long, locked-away conversations they have.

Margery is getting stranger each day. I don't like the effect she has on Ralph and Lizzie, either. She never raises her voice to them yet they seem afraid of her. To be honest, I wish she'd go away.

Last Monday, something happened that cured me completely of my old attraction to her. It was the queerest thing. I had returned from town, walked into my room and found Margery standing beside my bureau, meticulously cleaning the hairs out of my hairbrush!!!

She was so engrossed in what she was doing that she didn't notice me at first. When at last I said, "What are you doing?" she froze for an instant, then recovered herself, smiled, and laid the hairbrush down. She said she was "tidying up." I told her that tidying up my hairbrush was miles away from the realm of her responsibility. She nodded, and without a word, whisked out the door past me.

I wish I had said more, although I don't know what it would have been. The incident made me feel so peculiar—outraged, frightened, sullied. What on earth was she up to?

In a way, it's a relief to have a reason to distrust her. I did anyway, so it makes an odd kind of sense. I'm not sure why, but I feel that she's actually dangerous. I don't feel safe from her anywhere except in the conservatory. For some reason, she never goes in there so I take refuge there whenever I can. In lieu of Vera, give me the company of the blessed plants—only among them can I find peace, and safely lose myself in my work.

"Rats," said Cindy to herself, for she turned the page but found that the two or three following pages had been torn from the notebook. Just when it was getting good, she moaned to herself.

But before she could think any more about it, she fell fast asleep.

Chapter Eight

On the Monday after the party, the Sperry family left for Washington, D.C. And by Wednesday, the day Janet had told them she would water the plants, she still did not feel well. The headache had lifted the morning after the party, but it had left a residue of heaviness in her limbs, as if to warn her that the pain had only suspended itself and would strike again if she moved too fast.

She slept until ten o'clock every morning and took a nap every afternoon. Her sleep was infested with poisonous dreams. She woke up tired and dissatisfied, wanting to sleep some more. When she wasn't sleeping, she just lay around. She had a paper to write for one of her classes, but she kept putting it off. Her parents began to worry about her and wanted her to see a doctor. She resisted, saying she just needed to relax. This was vacation, after all.

But she couldn't lie to herself. Something was wrong, and it was getting worse. Nothing in the waking world seemed worth doing any more. This lethargy frightened her. It was like a formless sogginess taking over, destroying her will. *What's happening to me?* she asked herself.

Janet had mixed feelings about entering the empty Sperry house. On the one hand, she wanted to recapture the excitement she had felt early on the night of the party, when she and Cindy had talked about the ghosts. Would they speak to her the way they spoke to Cindy? On the other hand, she felt something like revulsion. Some strange voice warned her to stay away. The two feelings were contradictory, yet somehow connected. *But that's crazy,* she thought. *Things can't be connected and not connected at the same time. I'm out of my gourd, that's all.*

Toward late afternoon, before she could talk herself out of it, she dragged herself out of her sleepiness, put on her shoes, and headed toward the living room.

Amy was watching television. Janet could see only the top of her head above the back of the gray sofa.

"I'm going over to the Sperrys' to water the plants," she told her. "Want to come?"

"No thanks," said Amy, with finality.

"Why not? Are you still scared?"

"I'm not scared, but I *am* right in the middle of watching this program. Why don't you watch it with me? Besides, I don't think you should go to that place."

"But I promised! If I don't go, the plants will dry."

Amy turned and looked at Janet over the back of the sofa. "Let the ghosts water the plants."

"Oh come *on*," Janet said, wanting to laugh but afraid it might make Amy mad. "If you're so worried about evil spirits, why don't you come along and protect me?"

"No, I don't want to go over there."

"Okay," said Janet, "but if the ghosts get me and drag me away to the funny farm, it's your fault."

"It'll be high time, that's for sure," said Amy, trying not to show Janet how truly frightened she was.

Outside, the sunshine stained everything with its late afternoon orange tint. Janet pedalled away fast. She felt a burst of energy—it was partly an urgency to get her job done before the sun set. As she rode along, she glanced down uneasily at the monstrous length of her shadow on the road. I only have about half an hour, she thought. She pushed hard and made it up the hill more easily than usual.

She felt the hulking presence of the house well before she could see it. Why did it seem so large today? It loomed dead ahead of her, dark amid its escort of trees. The orange sun was about to slide down the tower. Cindy's white curtains hung motionless. All the doors and windows were closed. There was no sound or movement anywhere. The house looked opaque. It seemed to be holding itself still on purpose.

She thought, *I don't want to go in there.*

Oh come on, it's just David and Diane's house.

They don't happen to be home right now. You came to do them a favor, so do it.

I don't want to go in there! It looks too quiet—as if it's glad they're gone.

Don't be a jerk! It's just an empty house.

But what else? Who else? Her head gave its warning throb, a hot, sharp one. *There's something terrible in there, something that's been waiting for a chance . . . I don't want to go in there! Please don't make me!*

But her feet marched up the walk, and across the porch to the front door. Her trembling hand took out the key and fitted it into the lock.

I could still go home, Tomorrow morning I can pay Amy five dollars to come back here with me, and we can do it together, easily, in broad daylight. . .

Now take it easy. You're just spooked. Nothing can possibly happen. Think how happy you'll be when you're finished and on your way home.

The front door swung open with a creak she'd never noticed before. She stepped into the front hall.

The last time she had been here, the whole downstairs had been full of her friends dancing to disco music. There had been food and candles and laughter. But now it felt as if all of that might have been a hundred years ago. The place felt abandoned, gloomy, and much too silent.

Did she imagine it or was there a bad smell in the air?

Okay, she told herself, let's see. Shall I water the downstairs plants first, or go up and do

91

Cindy's? The thought of climbing the stairs to the tower made her feel strange. Suddenly, while she stood there shivering, she heard the door creak behind her. She turned just in time to see it click shut.

Why did it do that? There's no breeze at all.

Never mind—just GO!

She switched on the chandelier and ran to the second floor. She turned on the light for the stairs to the third floor and continued to run up. The skin along her spine crawled with the feeling that something was following her.

When she reached the third floor, she filled the plastic jug and made the rounds of the plants in the empty room. She felt calmer now. Then she refilled the jug, and started up the stairs to the tower.

As her foot touched the first step, she halted. There was a line of light coming from under Cindy's door. How could that be? Cindy wouldn't have left it on. But Janet remembered noticing from the outside that the tower windows were dark. What was going on? Who could be in there? Were they waiting for her? But before another second passed, she decided that no matter who or what it was, she was not going to deal with it. She'd go straight home and have her father call the police. She was about to tiptoe away when she realized what the light was, and laughed out loud. Of course, you dummy! she thought. Boldly she went up and opened the door.

Dark yellow light from the setting sun flooded the room and streamed across the floor. It was the sliver of it shining under the door that had looked like electric light.

So much for irrational terror, she thought. She was so relieved that she sang as she watered the avocado tree and the spider plants. All sense of forboding evaporated. By the time she was through, the light was beginning to fade. She left the room and bounced down the tower stairs, singing loudly as she went. But just as she was about to go down to the second floor, her tune was cut short. She stopped dead in her tracks and froze.

Someone is walking around down there.

A board creaked. She stood perfectly still, but heard no more. Deciding she must have imagined it, she took a few cautious steps down the stairs.

There it is again! The creaking, and *another* sound! Some kind of low-pitched, sobbing hiss.

She froze again, her hand tight on the bannister. Terror made her body contract.

From below there was silence again, and then, faintly, the sound of a drawer being closed.

I'm trapped. There's no way I can get down past it. Her heart beat as if it would club her to death. *Whatever's down there heard me singing.*

She felt a tide of surly, frustrated malevolence flowing up the stairs toward her. *I've felt that before! Where?*

She knew that while she was standing there, paralyzed, the sun was setting. Soon it would be dark.

Silence. For a few minutes, all was quiet. See? she said to herself, nothing. There had been no noise for a few minutes. *But the bad feeling is still there!*

It's just your imagination, your panic playing tricks on you. Didn't Cindy tell you that ghosts are harmless? Just go on down. You can't stay up here all night.

Quickly and quietly she ran down the stairs, pausing just a second to switch off the light. She sped along the gallery and down the front hall. At the foot of the stairs she rested, comforted by the bright glow of the chandelier.

She wanted to slip out the front door and run home, but there were more plants to water. She couldn't leave without doing that—she certainly didn't want to come back and do it in the morning, and she'd never be able to face Mr. Sperry if any of his plants died simply because she had gotten spooked. Anyway, she reassured herself, there had not been any more noises since she had come downstairs . . .

She headed into the conservatory. Maybe no one will ever know it, she thought, but I deserve a medal for this. Once there, she filled the water can, then took it into the living room and watered the plants there. The job was almost done.

She was about to return to the conservatory when she heard it again—the creaking upstairs and the voice—louder, this time. A low-pitched rasping whine, like the noise a dog makes when it wrestles with a bone.

And now there was unmistakably a smell of decay.

She set the watering can down in the middle of

the living room carpet and headed for the front door. *That's it—enough's enough. I've had it! I'm going home. Maybe Dad can stop by tomorrow to water the plants in the conservatory. Anyway, I feel sick.*

When she got to the hall, the bright light of the chandelier suddenly went out. She ran to the door and pulled the big brass knob, but it was stuck! The door was locked.

The smell of decay was nearly overpowering.

She turned. Something moving in the gallery had caught her eye. She looked up and saw, in the twilight, a black-robed, hooded figure. As it began to rush down the stairs, it made an angry whining noise and ground its teeth. Ahead of it, aimed at her alone, flowed a sharp, stinging malice.

In the next split second, her thoughts going at 78 rpm, she wondered if she should try the front door again or if she should run through the dining room into the kitchen and out the back door. Or, maybe she could get out through the cellar. But then, suddenly, obeying what seemed like a crazy, doomed impulse, she turned and ran back through the living room into the conservatory.

What are you doing? her reason yelled at her. *You'll be trapped!*

The black-clad figure was close behind her. The reek of its rottenness engulfed her nostrils.

The dark orange rays of the setting sun were shining into the conservatory onto the glossy green leaves of the plants, printing their shadows onto the concrete floor. The air was soft and sweet. Janet breathed it gratefully, shut her eyes for a short second, and crashed into something. She opened her eyes with a start—oh, it was only the stepladder. Suddenly, she felt calm and strong. Her judgment was crystal clear. She seized the stepladder and turned to face her attacker.

Night had entered the living room. Against its darkness she couldn't make out what was trying to hurl itself into the conservatory. The foul smell that flowed in was almost unbearable. Then her eyes adjusted to the dying light, and she saw the darkly wrapped figure pressed against the empty space of the doorway. Claw-like hands reached for her and then withdrew into the darkness of the cloak. Within the folds of the hood glowed a pale, half-decayed face. Its mottled green flesh hung in softening strips from the bone. Its eyes were black holes. Something phosphorescent squirmed in their depths.

It reached and reached for her, but could not touch her. Then it spoke, its voice a dry, toneless hiss. The words flew at her on gusts of sickening stench. "Pretty smart, aren't you! You know you're safe in there—for now. But not for long. You'll be out of my way soon. He's not so clever. He's not safe from me anywhere. He won't get away this time! Soon he'll be mine forever!"

Without realizing what she was doing, Janet lifted the stepladder and with three times the strength she thought she possessed, swung it around and smashed through the glass window of the conservatory. Quickly, she scrambled through the jagged hole.

Once outside, the certainty she had just felt so

strongly began to weaken. The shivering hand of panic grabbed the back of her neck but she shook it off. She had to stay calm in order to get herself home.

The sun had just set. Darkness was already thick beneath the bushes and trees. She made herself walk as casually as possible to the gateposts. Somehow she knew that the thing in the house would not pursue her, so she was able to restrain the impulse to run wildly away.

Although she was beginning to tremble, she calmly walked her bicycle down the driveway under the shadow of the trees. When she reached the main road, she switched on the bike's headlamp and began to coast down the long hill.

As the bicycle picked up speed, her trembling increased. Her ordeal was over and the gift of superhuman clarity and power that had gotten her through it was waning. Her calm drained away. As the wheels spun faster and faster, shock spread its tide of numbness throughout her body. Retroactive horror squealed gibberish in her ears.

She was never able to remember exactly how she got home. By the time she reached the foot of the hill, everything had become a blur of pain and panic. Her head throbbed. Every hammerstroke of its pounding drove blackness deeper into her consciousness. She barely had enough strength and wit to manage riding her bicycle. Somehow, she reached the driveway, put the bike away in the garage, and made it in the front door.

Amy and Mr. and Mrs. Gray heard her screaming as soon as she walked in. It was a long, hard, high-pitched scream. They came running and found her standing in the hall, her eyes open wide and staring at nothing. She screamed until she ran out of breath, then she filled her lungs and screamed again—that high, hard, steady, unchanging note. Amy burst into tears. When Mr. Gray took Janet by the shoulders, her scream shattered into smithereens of sobbing. She threw herself into her father's arms and clung to him. Then she reached for her mother. She wanted them all to hold her at once.

They managed to get her upstairs. Her mother put her to bed while her father telephoned the doctor. When he came back she was under the covers, shivering violently, even with the extra blanket her mother had brought in. Still sobbing, she clutched her mother's hands. Mr. Gray gave her a shot of whiskey. In a little while, her trembling lessened. She tried to talk but the horror of what she had to say brought the sobs back again.

"My head—my head—" she kept saying. The pain filled her whole skull. It was driving her into unconsciousness. She wanted desperately to tell her family what had happened, to unload the terror, before she passed out.

In fragments, in gasps, she told them. "At the Sperrys' a corpse—rotten, stinking, in black— chased me. It wanted to kill me," she said. "I broke out through a window." She knew, as she let herself dissolve into nothingness, that they would never believe her.

They couldn't. They looked at each other,

shocked. The only possible explanation for what they had just heard was that Janet was suffering from a nervous collapse.

After examining her briefly, the doctor called an ambulance.

Mr. Gray called the police and asked them to check the Sperry place. In a few hours, they called back to say they had found nothing wrong except a broken window in the conservatory, a watering can overturned in the living room, and the trace of a bad smell—maybe a dead rat, they thought.

The next day, Mr. Gray arranged to have the window repaired.

Chapter Nine

Even after an exciting day of sightseeing, Cindy could think of nothing she'd rather do than continue reading Clayton's journal. The entry dated Monday, May 17, 1907 began:

The greatest day of my life! We're to be married. I'm foolish with joy! I'm so happy I can't sleep. Life feels right-side-up at last.

Vera sent word yesterday that she had recovered, so this morning I rode down to visit her. The air was saturated with the fragrance of flowers all blooming at once and the music of birds. We sat there and drank it all in. There was nothing to say; the pleasure of being together would have been enough. But finally I spoke. I said, "By the way, my sweet, when shall we be married?"

She didn't bat an eye but as cool as you please, answered, "Oh, I don't know—next month would be all right, I suppose."

"But that's June. Do we want people to think we're the slaves of tradition?"

"Oh, let them think what they want. A little collision with tradition won't do us any harm." Then she looked at me, her eyes all agleam, and burst out with a laughing yell and threw herself into my arms.

Everybody is overjoyed. Cathy especially—it's good to see her so cheerful. I think she'll be glad to have me out of the way, fond of me though she is.

I guess I should not have said that *everybody* is overjoyed. Margery isn't, not that I expected her to be. Actually, since I found her in my bedroom the other day, she's hardly looked at me. When Cathy told her my news, she just said, "Oh, congratulations." She didn't even pause on her way upstairs.

This coming Saturday evening we are going to have a dinner party, just our two families, to announce the engagement formally and celebrate and make plans.

Cindy dropped the book in her lap and rubbed her eyes. Just at that moment, David and Diane walked in.

"Oh, no," they groaned in unison. "You didn't bring the ghosts down here did you?"

Cindy simmered silently. *When* would they understand?

David flopped on the bed. "So what's happening in spooksville tonight, little one?"

"It just so happens," Cindy said, "that I was reading a very interesting part about Margery."

101

"Ah," said David, "our favorite disappearing lady."

"Oh come on, David, give the kid a chance," said Diane. "What about Margery?"

"You know, she spoiled Clayton's engagement dinner."

"Big deal," smirked David.

Honestly, Cindy thought to herself, when will her brother ever grow up?

"What happened, Cin?" asked Diane.

"Well, apparently everyone was having a great time. Vera's whole family was there, as well as all of the Dexters, but Margery seemed particularly quiet. When they toasted the new couple, Margery didn't even say a word."

"How terrifying," David said sarcastically.

Cindy ignored her brother's remark. "All of a sudden, right out of the blue, Margery started telling Cathy how terrible it was to be alone. She started saying awful things about how Cathy would feel when she 'lost' Clayton."

"That's weird," said Diane.

"Yeah, I know. Listen to this." Cindy picked up the dusty leather notebook and began to read out loud.

"Think of how you'll feel, Cathy, when their honeymoon coach has just driven out of sight. For the first time in your life, you'll know what it is to be abandoned. Without *him*, without your twin, how will you know yourself? You'll be like a person who looks into the mirror and sees no reflection coming to meet her. You'll feel wispy, useless, like a wraith—"

"She must have been some spooky lady," said Diane when Cindy finished reading.

"Yeah," Cindy agreed, "and Clayton writes that everyone was listening to Margery—apparently she was talking loud enough for the whole room to hear . . ."

"Read some more," Diane interrupted.

Cindy lifted the book and began:

"One by one, people stopped their jolly foolishness and tuned in to these abominable words. At last the whole party was paralyzed with horror and embarrassment. Cathy sank before our eyes and her face grew pale and sad. Her eyes clouded over and she wilted in her chair like a plant whose roots are being eaten by worms."

"That's a strange image," David commented.

"I thought you weren't interested," said Cindy, but before her brother could reply, she continued to read:

"I think I might have reached across the table and hit Margery, but suddenly Vera stood up. She was very pale. Her eyes flashed and she sternly looked down at Margery.

"What are you trying to do to us?" she said. Her voice shook slightly. "Why are you trying to spoil our happiness? All we want is to make our lives and the lives of those we love as happy as possible. You seem to wish us only misery and weakness.

"Now listen, Margery, Cathy is and will always be Clay's beloved twin sister. To me she is a dear friend, and soon, I'm happy to say, she'll be my sister as well. My only sister—I have no other.

What on earth makes you think that we would ever let her be lonely and miserable?

"'You pretend to be pitiful but you're not. You're strong. If you've come through the great hardships you say you have, you must be very strong indeed—yet you try to transform our joy into guilt and worry. Is it to create company for your own misery? You shouldn't be so silly. Use your strength like a plant does and turn your face to the sun. Then you will be happy.'"

"Bravo!" said David. "Now there's a woman after my own heart."

Just the words Clayton would have used, thought Cindy. "But that's not all," she said. "After that, Clayton wrote that Margery seemed changed—wait, here it is." She read on:

"Margery seemed emaciated, as if the sound of Vera's words had worn her flesh away. Her face took on a greenish pallor. She left her place at the table and thrust her face close to Vera's. She spoke in a slow, guttural rasp: 'Happiness! You'll never be happy! You won't marry Clay. You're going to die and your precious "sister" Cathy will lose her mind. Clay is mine! He belongs to me—and some day, sooner or later, everyone will know it!'"

"Wow!" said Diane.

"Clayton was crushed," Cindy added, "and Vera seemed about to collapse."

"Margery sounds like such a horrible *thing*, or person or ghost . . . or *something*. I don't know what to call her."

"Certainly not a girl I'd like to invite to a party," quipped David.

"Ha-ha," said Diane.

Cindy didn't say a word. All she wished was that her brother and sister would go away and leave her with her books.

Chapter Ten

Janet was dreaming. All through the dream she repeated, "This is no dream."

In the dream she was so sleepy that it took all her strength to open her eyes. She longed to keep them closed, to surrender to the total blackout, but if she did that she was afraid she would die. She forced herself to keep lifting her tombstone eyelids, giving herself a scum-lined sliver of space to see through.

All around her was a clammy fog, stained with dark brown twilight. An ugly smell emanated from the ground and mingled with the fog; the thick moistness congealed into sickly shadows, vaguely human in form. They drifted close to her and whispered nonsense in her ears.

The place was maddeningly familiar, but something was missing. Some important landmark was not there and she couldn't remember what it had been. It was important that she remember, so she threw all her strength into keeping her eyes open.

But she loathed where she was and wanted only to slip into the comfort of a dreamless death.

Forcing herself to gaze into the clearing where the missing thing was supposed to be, she saw the earth begin to shift and swell, like infected skin erupting into a boil. The hump of earth cracked open. The stink suddenly became so strong that Janet retched. She backed into the rough, wet arms of a big tree. The tree held her up solidly. She was grateful, because her legs were worthless and her head a cauldron of agony. Without the tree, she would have collapsed altogether at the horror of what happened next.

Something was struggling to climb out of the sick earth, trying to free itself, staggering to its feet. It was a decaying corpse, glowing green with the phosphorescence of bacteria that were decomposing it. Its rough exit from the earth had ripped chunks and strips of softened flesh off its frame. Guts spilled through the gaps. Driven by some terrible need, it came toward Janet. As it moved, it tried to repair itself by gathering up its rotten guts and pouring them back into its cavity. It plastered handfuls of flesh back onto its bones. Its face came closer and closer. Its eye sockets were nests of white worms.

When it had come within a hand's breadth, it stopped. She heard the brown air wheeze and gurgle through the crevices of its broken body. Then it breathed its heavy stench directly into her nostrils. She wanted to fall down and die, but the tree supported her. Then she noticed some green plants starting to grow around the corpse's feet.

They shot up out of the ground, taller and taller, and wrapped themselves around the body, pulling it down and away from her. Snarling, the corpse fought with them, using its bony hands for a sickle to chop them down.

The plants fell and turned to fire and sprang up hot red and yellow. The wet ground hissed. Steam rose and mingled with the cold fog. The flames climbed higher and spread wider and expanded into an enormous blaze. Janet was not burned, but the corpse vanished into the flames. When the steam cleared, she saw that the fire was consuming the frame of a house. Then she knew where she was.

The house burned to the ground. The flames died and the brown fog moved in again. The earth heaved and the corpse erupted from it and came toward her again. Once more she smelled its rottenness and felt the piercing malice of its intent. Again the plants grew up and seized it, were beaten down, and became flames.

The dream repeated itself over and over. Each time, the corpse came a little closer to her and blew a stronger storm of stench. The pain sank deeper into her brain. Her yearning for sleep was becoming impossible to resist.

Just as she was about to let her eyes close, a thin blade of wind touched her cheek, cutting the stench with the scent of herbs. A woman's voice sounded in her mind, a low, sweet voice—she couldn't catch the words but she recognized the tone. Then it was gone, and so was the odor of herbs. She felt refreshed and strong enough to keep her eyes open for a little while longer.

The corpse returned. The dream repeated itself.

On Friday evening, as soon as the Sperrys returned from Washington, Mr. Sperry went to the conservatory to check on his plants. In a few minutes he came back, a look of alarm on his face.

"The plants are almost bone dry," he said. "They haven't been watered. The watering can is in the middle of the living room floor. And the strangest thing is that there's a brand new pane of glass in the conservatory."

"All my plants got watered, Dad," Cindy said. She had already run upstairs to see them.

David went to the phone and dialed Janet's number. They heard him ask to speak to her. Then his face changed and he just listened. At last he spoke. "When can we see her?" he asked.

When he hung up, his face was white. "Janet's in the hospital," he said. "That was her dad. He says they don't know what it is yet. It looks like some kind of nervous collapse. She came over here Wednesday to water the plants and when she got home she was in hysterics. She said she'd been attacked here by some rotten-smelling person in a black cloak who ran downstairs and chased her into the conservatory. She smashed the window with the stepladder to get away. She made it home and then collapsed. She's been unconscious ever since. Her mom's staying at the hospital with her."

"Oh, no!" everybody said, looking at each other in horror.

"I can't believe it," said Mr. Sperry. "Janet's the healthiest person I know."

"She's been having awful headaches lately," said David. "I kept begging her to see a doctor, but she didn't want to."

"But a creature like that—could some derelict have gotten into the house?" said Mrs. Sperry, looking around in alarm.

"Janet's dad says he sent the police over, but they didn't find any signs of a break in," said David.

"She must have been hallucinating," said Mrs. Sperry.

Mr. Sperry called back Mr. Gray to hear for himself what had happened, then he called the police for their report. Meanwhile, the twins and Cindy went through the house looking for signs of disturbance. They found nothing until they went into David's room on the second floor, when they all stopped and wrinkled their noses in disgust.

"There must be a dead animal somewhere," said Diane.

David looked under the furniture and in the closet, but found nothing. "A mouse must have died in the wall again," he said. "We really do have to get a cat." He opened up all the windows.

"It's not a mouse," said Cindy.

It was the first time she had spoken since they'd heard about Janet. Her tone was so grave that they both turned and stared at her. She sat down on David's plaid bedspread and looked back at them, calmly but defiantly.

"So what is it?" Diane asked her.

110

"Look, would you two come up to my room after supper?" she said. "I have to show you something. It's really important. But," she continued, looking at David, "you have to promise to take it seriously and not make fun."

Something in her tone and manner commanded their attention.

"You've got it, Cindy," David promised.

So, after supper the three of them climbed the stairs to Cindy's room.

The twins sat down on the fuzzy white carpet while Cindy rummaged in her half-unpacked suitcase and pulled something out. It was an old-fashioned leatherbound notebook.

"This," she said, riffling the pages, which the twins saw were written on in faded, purplish-brown ink, "is the missing volume of Clayton Dexter's diary, the one that covers the time after Clayton married Vera. It goes up to the day he died and tells the whole story."

"Where did you find it?" asked Diane.

"Well," Cindy answered, "you know that little closet under the tower stairs, the one with the door that sticks? I've tried to open that door hundreds of times. It was so tight I thought it must be nailed shut. I was a little scared, because I kept thinking there might be a skeleton in it. But then, a couple of weeks ago, I dreamed that Clayton took me by the hand and led me to that closet. I could tell by the way he looked at me that there was something in that closet he wanted me to get at. In the morning I went down and it opened, easy as pie! I found the book inside. I finished reading it while we were in Washington, and I want to read it to you now because I think then we'll understand what's happened to Janet and what smells bad around here."

"Read away," said David.

Cindy opened the book to the entry dated Monday, May 24, 1907, and read:

"Vera is very ill. She doesn't know me. She's wasted away—she hasn't eaten for days—and she looks pale and talks incoherently. When I hold her hands and call her, she looks through me with vacant eyes, murmuring and moaning, as if she were in the grip of horrible dreams.

"Once she did awaken enough to recognize me. She tried to throw herself into my arms, as if she wanted to be saved from something, but she didn't have the strength to raise herself off the pillow. She looked into my eyes and I could see that she was making a desperate effort to come to the surface of the swamp of a nightmare she was drowning in, to clear her vision, to convince me that she was rational.

"'Margery,' she kept saying. 'Don't trust her. Send her away, get rid of her, as soon as you can. She's not human. She's a fiend.'

"I told her that Mama and Papa have already given Margery notice, but at that, Vera closed her eyes and moved her head impatiently.

"'That's not enough,' she whispered. 'She'll always return, even from the grave, unless she's completely destroyed.' Then she sighed, as if relieved, and fell asleep.

"I couldn't believe I'd heard her right. Destroy

Margery completely? What can she mean? Her words haunt me. I can't deny it—some sixth sense is telling me there may be a ghastly truth in them. I feel as if I could strangle in this net of confusion."

"This gives me the creeps," said Diane.

Cindy ignored her and began reading the entry for Friday, May 28:

"Vera is much better! When she looked at me there were tears in her eyes. I asked her why, and she said it was because she was so glad to be alive and with me. I couldn't bring myself to ask her to explain her terrible words about Margery.

"Monday, May 31:

"How to begin. I don't want to write it. To see it in writing will be like hearing the door of my jail cell clang shut.

"Vera is dead. I am sentenced to life in solitary confinement."

Cindy paused and looked at the twins. They sat on the floor, hugging their knees. Diane had tears in her eyes. David twisted the white fibers of the rug between his fingers. A thin wind was beginning to moan and pry at the tower windows. She continued to read:

"Later.

"I must write about how it happened. The horrible, incredible truth must be recorded exactly. It would be no use telling the truth to family and friends and the police. They'd never believe it. Cathy and I would be locked up in the insane asylum.

"To begin, on Saturday after lunch, Cathy and I got ready to take Vera for the drive we had promised. I hitched the horse to the chaise and brought him around to the front door. I climbed up and took the reins, and sat there waiting for Cathy, who I thought was just putting on her hat.

"She didn't come out and didn't come out and I was about to go and yell for her to hurry up when the front door opened and out came Margery, all dressed for a drive!

"I was not very glad to see her, to put it mildly. She told me Cathy was tired and had asked her if she could go instead. I found this hard to believe and was about to drive on alone, but then she looked up at me in her most beguiling way and I couldn't resist. She pleaded that she'd soon be gone for good, and claimed she wanted to apologize to Vera for the scene she had caused at our dinner. To my shame, I fell for it. Up into the chaise she climbed, and off we went."

Cindy saw David and Diane exchange glances but she didn't say a word. When David saw her looking at him, he blushed and urged her to go on.

Cindy continued reading:

"I found out later what she had done with Cathy. She had spent the morning bending Cathy's ear again, talking about how dismal the orphanage was and hinting that she wanted to be forgiven and invited to stay on as Cathy's companion after I was to be married.

"And just as Cathy was going out the door, Margery asked her to help bring up a small packing box from the basement. Cathy agreed but while they were down there, Margery slipped upstairs and locked the cellar door behind her!

Then she grabbed her hat and came out to me! Cathy waited there in the dark for two hours before someone finally heard her calling."

"She sure had a case on Clayton, didn't she?" It was Diane who spoke.

"Yeah, there's definitely something weird about it," murmured David.

"Wait until you hear *how* weird," cautioned Cindy. She picked up her book again and continued reading:

"Vera waited for us on her front porch. I'll never forgive myself for the look on her face when she saw Margery with me instead of Cathy. Her expression of radiant gladness simply ceased. I'd never seen her look like that before.

"My own heart sank as if a stone had knocked a hole in it. Regret and forboding flooded me. I could hardly stand the sound of my voice as I explained to her that Margery wanted to be forgiven and to say goodbye.

"I settled her next to Margery and climbed onto the box, feeling wretched. I drove down the street and entered the park. I could hear Margery's voice murmuring behind me but I couldn't make out what she was saying. From Vera I heard nothing.

"I took the road around the duck pond. It was covered with children's toy sailboats—a lovely sight, like a flock of white butterflies—and I turned around to point it out to Vera.

"What I saw made me sick with rage. Vera was lying back in the corner of the chaise with her head fallen to one side and her eyes closed.

Margery was leaning over her, holding her face in her hands and she appeared to be breathing directly into her nostrils."

"Into her nostrils?" screamed Diane. "That's gross!"

"Be quiet," David said. "Let Cindy go on."

Cindy continued:

"I yelled, 'Let go!' and taking the reins in my left hand, I swung back at Margery with my right. It would have been a good clout, but I couldn't reach her. I faced front again and turned the chaise around. Without delay we raced straight back to the McNultys'.

"I pulled up at the front door and yelled for Andy, their hired man. Then I swung around and gathered Vera into my arms. Margery sat beside her, braced against the back of the seat. She was pale and scrawny, her eyes vicious, her teeth uncovered like a cornered rat's. I managed to get Vera out of the chaise. Then, heartbroken at the weight of her hopelessness, I roared at Margery: 'Get away from us—get out of our lives! Today! If I ever catch you, I swear I'll kill you!'

"Vera was unconscious. I carried her indoors and up to her bedroom, where I gave her to her mother. I rode for the doctor. He promised to come as soon as he could and then I went to the ironworks to tell George McNulty what had happened.

"When I returned, Vera was in a deep coma. I sat beside her and held her hand. Before, she had raved and thrashed around, occasionally regaining enough awareness to recognize me. Now she lay

116

motionless, hardly even breathing. Her hand in mine felt like an empty glove.

"I gazed at her and pleaded with all my soul for her to come back to me, but she never moved. Her face was colorless, shadows filled the hollows around her eyes. It was clear that she was dying. Her mother was with me at her bedside, and soon George came home and joined us.

"When the doctor came, he shook his head. He couldn't find what was wrong, and all he said was that he didn't think she'd last long. It could be hours or a few days. Her parents were so distraught that he advised them to get some rest. I insisted on staying up with Vera, and promised to call them if anything happened.

"The hours went by. I was beginning to doze off when I heard her draw one deep breath, and then another. Her hand moved slightly, then grasped mine. I saw her eyelids flicker and her lips move. She opened her eyes and looked straight into mine.

"Her gaze was clear, perfectly focused, and full of love. As if trying her voice to see if it still worked, she spoke my name. I hushed her, but she drew another breath, and said, 'It's all right. I know I'm dying. And I know I have enough strength to tell you what I must tell you. Sweetheart, you mustn't blame yourself for this. It isn't your fault. We've all been under the same evil spell.'"

Cindy stopped reading and stretched. The rising wind sang as it swayed the treetops outside.

David moved over to lean against the door. He

felt like having something solid behind his back to lean against. Without the sound of Cindy's voice to fill it, the room seemed too quiet. It wasn't a silence due to some absence, but something that was being deliberately quiet.

"I don't like this at all," groaned Diane. "The whole thing gives me the willies. There is something really disgusting about the whole thing."

Cindy and David did not answer her.

"Don't either of you feel it, too?" Diane persisted. "I feel like something dead is in here."

David approached Diane and put his arm around her. "I know what you mean, but just try to calm down and let Cindy finish."

David noticed the silence again. In fact, he was still aware of it when Cindy resumed reading Vera's last words to Clayton:

"'Clayton, I've been having such revolting dreams that I can hardly bear to tell them to you, but I must, for it is the only way you and Cathy will be saved. For me it is too late. Listen to what I've learned from these dreams.

"'Margery is not human. She is neither alive nor dead. She belongs to a species of creature related to the vampire, a spectre who refuses to die a natural death. By means of magical deceptions, it preserves its flesh through countless lifetimes. It appears to die many deaths, but each time it rises and dresses itself in the semblance of a new body, which is actually the same body that was born two hundred, five hundred, or a thousand years ago.

"'Such a creature begins its existence as a normal human infant. But at some point in its life, it gives in to the belief that its soul is bound to die along with its body. It has no understanding that life goes on, even after you die. Thus, it falls prey to the deepest despair there is.

"'Unable to trust the power of life to conduct its individuality beyond the grave, it calls upon evil powers to help it preserve its flesh forever. But like a tree that refuses to shed its leaves, a soul that tries to reverse the laws of nature and live in such an abominably maintained body becomes an abomination itself—desperate, insatiably hungry, inconsolably envious. It is like a rose without water; all its powers of love and humor dry up. It loses the very thing it really wanted to save—its humanity, its love of life—and changes from a human being into an *it*, a walking corpse. The horror of it is that such a creature may physically look breathtakingly beautiful. You'd never know, to look at it, what hideousness its beauty disguises.

"'In order to maintain the illusion that it is a living human being, this creature must be able to assure itself that it is real, that it is loved. It dreads being alone, for then it would no longer be able to fool itself. Having no life of its own, it feeds on the lives of others. That is why Margery needs you. She must have you only for herself. She needs you to convince her that she is alive. She'll destroy me and Cathy and anyone else who stands in her way.'"

"Uh oh," said Diane. "I think I know what's coming."

"What do you mean?" asked David, with fear in his eyes.

"It's obvious where this is heading. Who does this creature remind you of?"

"Pass me that quilt, would you?" was all David could say in reply. "I'm cold."

Diane passed it to him. He wrapped himself up in it and huddled against the door.

Cindy read on:

"'My dream didn't show me how many hundreds of years ago Margery's natural birth occurred, but it did reveal how she became involved with your family.

"'Fifty years ago, on the site where this house is, stood a different house. A small family lived in it—a husband and wife and their son. One day when the son was about twelve years old, a poor orphan girl came to their door.

"'The kind-hearted people took her in. But she was a strange girl and from the beginning, she demanded the boy's constant attention. It seemed as if she had come to the house knowing that he was there, wanting only to capture him.

"'Although the boy liked her at first, he soon began to avoid her and as time went by, he resisted her domination more and more.'"

Cindy looked up from her book when she heard David sigh.

"Are you sure any of this has to do with Janet? I don't see the point," he complained.

"Just be patient," she answered dramatically.

"I'm not sure I want to hear this," said Diane as she huddled next to her brother, watching Cindy as she continued to read:

"'When this young boy grew to be a young man,

he fell in love with a young woman. This made the orphan girl sour. She called upon her powers as a witch. She was—is—a mighty one. One of her special tricks was to steal bits of the young man's hair and weave spells into it to pacify him and paralyze his will.'"

"His *hair*!" shouted Diane.

"Big deal," said David.

"But don't you remember, David? Mirella! At the party!"

David gasped as Cindy read on:

"'As soon as he became engaged, his fiancée mysteriously died. Her death left him despondent. He didn't care what happened to himself. He fell deeper and deeper into the abyss of the witch's power until he was on the verge of surrendering to her.

"'Then one night, after everyone was asleep, the witch crept into the young man's room to cut another lock of his hair. As she leaned over him, a drop of hot wax from her candle splashed onto his cheek. He awoke suddenly and startled her so much that she dropped the candle. Within seconds, the entire bedroom was ablaze. The young man seized the girl by the wrist and dragged her from the burning house.

"'Once outside, the lad let go of the girl. With a triumphant shriek, she ran back into the flames. He could not follow her. It looked as if she must certainly have died.

"'Fire is supposed to destroy witches, but this was neither an ordinary fire nor an ordinary witch. Seeing that her spells had failed to enslave the young man, she had created the fire herself and leaped into it deliberately, knowing that she could keep her evil power intact, reconstitute her dead flesh into the semblance of another living body, and return to the world to capture another man.

"'She did return. In my dream, I saw the witch-girl shrivel and melt in the flames and vanish under the ashes.

"'Three nights later, I had another dream where I saw her—or rather, *it*—climb from the burned timbers of the house—a shrunken, blackened, brittle shape, tottering through the ruins under a full moon.

"'It fed on the moonlight, basking in it as we do in the sunshine. As I watched, it lifted its destroyed face up to the blue-green rays and grew steady and strong once again. Soon it was moving with the same speed and power as it had in life.

"'I saw it walk to the graveyard and continue straight to where there were two identical gravestones. Then it kneeled down and began to pull up the sod, digging madly, pulling up great chunks of earth with its charred hands. Finally, it had dug itself a deep and narrow grave which it then leaped into as gracefully as a cat. I saw the earth which it had piled up beside the grave pour back in. The chunks of sod fitted themselves together over the raw earth like the pieces of a puzzle. The two gravestones looked just as they had before. Nobody would have guessed there was a third grave in there.

"'Then, in my dream, time passed. But many years later, the earth cracked and out of the ground climbed the charred figure looking just as she had when she leapt in.

"'With delicate stealth, it gathered handfuls of the tall, dead grasses that grew around the gravestones. The grasses disappeared between its fingers and became a long black hooded cape. Then, it lifted its featureless face to the moon and began a whining, howling incantation. As it chanted, its body took on the shape of a woman, with hands and face that were white and smooth, as if covered with real skin. Blond hair grew out of its head. Then it began a slow, wild, stamping dance, pressing the broken earth down over the place where the grave had been.'"

"Mirella!" David gasped.

"I thought you'd be interested in this," chirped Cindy.

"Don't get wise, little one. Just go on!" David snapped.

Cindy picked up where she had left off:

"'The moon grazed the treetops at the edge of the graveyard. In its light, I saw how the ghastly corpse that had emerged from the ground an hour before had now become a perfectly ordinary-looking, quite lovely human form. No one would have hesitated to offer her his protection. Except for the unnatural strength in her movements and a dreadful power and quickness like that of a starving animal, she looked completely normal.

"'As the moon was crossed by the bare treetops, she stalked swiftly between the graves. By dawn she was well on her way to the orphanage. The rest you know.'"

"It was Margery!" shrieked Diane.

"Good work, Dr. Watson," said Cindy.

"But the horrible thing now," said David as he struggled to keep his voice steady, "the horrible thing now is that . . . is that . . ."

"That's right, David," said Cindy. "Margery never died. There's only one way to kill a thing like that, to put an end to such an unnatural destructive force."

"Well, don't keep us in suspense little sister! What is it?"

"Plants."

"*Plants*?" David repeated incredulously.

"Listen," Cindy commanded as she finished reading Vera's story:

"'Green plants are toxic to Margery. The power of life to regenerate itself, which she denies, is so strong that she can't bear to be near it. The herbs that protect against witchcraft are fatal to her. Not only will they destroy her, but they will heal most of the harm that she has done.

"'Take some vervain, also some Saint Johnswort and some bay laurel, and make a strong tea. When it's cool, drink it and give a good draught of it to Cathy. It will dissolve the evil spell. Cathy has been deeply wounded. She may always be susceptible to melancholy after this, but if you act right away you can save her from fatal madness. After she's had a drink, let her rest.

"'Then find Margery and before she realizes what you're doing, pour the tea over her head. Be prepared for a horror—she will disintegrate into a corpse before your very eyes.

"'You must be sure to make the tea secretly. If Margery finds out what you are up to and that you are on to her, she will escape you by committing suicide. Sooner or later, she will rise from her grave to repeat the cycle all over again.'"

Cindy closed the book.

"What are we going to do?" asked David. His voice rattled in his throat.

Nobody answered.

Chapter Eleven

Cindy looked up. Her eyes were dark. She was listening, not to the wind outside, but to the quality of the silence inside. The only one to acknowledge it, she gave a funny little smile and minuscule salute with her eyebrows.

"Cindy," Diane bravely asked, "what ever happened?"

"Well, Clayton made the tea and he and Cathy drank some of it."

"But what about Margery?" David asked.

"Do you really want to know?" asked Cindy. "It's gruesome."

"Yes, go ahead."

"Well, Clayton was carrying a pot of the tea to Margery's room when all of a sudden, he felt assaulted by a rotten smell. He wheeled back and just then, a black-clad figure burst through Margery's door and knocked him against the wall. The tea splashed all over the place, but the figure leaped clear of it and ran up the stairs. The next thing Clayton heard was Cathy's screams and then, well, wait, let me find the page." Cathy riffled through the book. "Here it is," she said, and began to read:

"I heard a hideous, unhuman, snarling screech, then a crash and the splinter of glass. Then, the thud of a body rolling down the steep roof and, finally, a splattering wallop as it hit the flagstones below.

"I ran to Cathy's room. The west window was gone and only a few pieces of glass were left around the edges. Cathy was speechless and rigid with shock. I ran to the window and leaned out, but I couldn't see past the edges of the roof to the ground. I dashed downstairs and out through the kitchen to the terrace. I saw a black heap on the flagstones. Nothing else. Wisps of foul-smelling mist rose from the heap and vanished into the air. The cloak was empty. There was nothing in it—no dead or injured woman, no body at all.

"I had failed.

"Despair hit me like a sledgehammer. I saw blackness. The ground lifted under me and I fainted."

David stood up, shedding the quilt. "I don't want to hear any more of this," he said.

Cindy and Diane looked at him and saw that his face was pale.

"You're freaked out," said Diane.

"You bet I am," he agreed. "I've had enough. I'm going downstairs." But he didn't leave. He just stood there, staring.

"Well," said Cindy, "there's no law that says

you have to hear any more."

But he still stood there, slightly trembling.

"I'll tell you what," said Diane. "I'll go down and make some hot chocolate."

"Oh, no," said David. "If one of us goes, all of us go."

"All right, all right," Diane said as she resumed her place by his side.

Cindy said, "Well, you know the rest, about how the town came to distrust the Dexters. I mean it really was peculiar, the broken window, black cape, and no body. It was really hard for Clayton and Cathy. Clayton nearly had a nervous breakdown."

"Okay, Cindy," David interrupted. "Enough about your ghosts."

"But David," Cindy persisted. "That's just it, that's the last thing. One night, Clayton and Cathy were drinking tea and they just knew that Vera was there. They felt her presence. They even heard her laugh. And that was the night Clayton sealed his journal and hid it under the stairs. He writes in the end that he hoped his words would help."

"But how?" cried Diane.

"Listen," Cindy said as she began to read Clayton's final words:

"Twice, now, the foul creature we knew as Margery has come to this spot and worked her evil upon those who live here. To this spot she will come the third time. When she does, this journal will be waiting. I hope that those who are being tormented will read it and save themselves and destroy the witch once and for all.

"I swear, by my love for Vera, that though we shall be dead, Cathy and I will return in spirit to make sure the journal is found and used. The ardent benevolence of our purpose will give us the power to accomplish it. Surely, if such a creature as Margery can survive death in order to carry out an evil task, we can survive death in order to defeat her."

Cindy closed the book. Her voice left a slowly fading imprint on the silence in the room. Outside, a gust of wind threw itself against the tower and rattled its windows angrily. David felt a coldness on the back of his neck.

He and Diane looked at each other. Diane was crying silently and David felt his own eyes beginning to fill up. He looked away, and clamped his jaw shut. But he trembled inside.

He thought of Janet far away in a hospital bed, with her temperature, blood pressure, and brain waves being monitored. He could envision a bottle of liquid nourishment hanging by her bed, seeping into her body through a needle in her vein—his Janet, lost in a swamp of nightmare, unable to tell anyone what the real trouble was, and with nobody near who would believe her even if she could tell them. How alone could anyone be? He bit his lip.

Diane breathed heavily. "So that explains Mirella! She's exactly like Margery! The way she looks and the things she says, the way she comes up so close and breathes in your face and bats her eyes, the way she can make you feel so depressed and guilty for being alive—and—the way she's always picking hairs off your clothes! No wonder she collected samples of everyone's hair! She is going to use them to cast spells on everyone!"

"It's good that she never got hold of Janet's hair, or Janet might be in much worse shape than she is right now—in other words, dead," said Cindy. "Mirella made Janet sick the same way she made Vera sick by breathing on her, poisoning her with her own dead breath."

"Ugh," said Diane. "Poor Janet!"

But David said, "Now wait, wait just a minute."

He felt torn. On the one hand, he saw Janet, her white hospital bed drifting further and further away, with nobody knowing she was lost. But on the other hand, with a pang of uncomfortable tenderness, he saw Mirella's face—the beautiful smoky eyes staring at him hungrily.

The journal had moved him to tears. But it had all been so long ago—could such things really happen in the modern world? Did the journal justify accusing poor Mirella of being a monster? Where was the proof?

"I'm not sure I can go along with this," he said. "Why blame Mirella for what this Margery creature did?"

"Oh David, come on!" exclaimed Diane.

"Blame isn't the point, David," said Cindy. There was such urgent, yet patient, wisdom in her young face that David and Diane were taken aback. "The point is," she continued, "there *is* something we can do for Janet that might save her life. It's a simple thing. Is there really any question about that?"

Once again, a vision flashed in David's mind of Mirella with her sultry face and knowing smile.

"If we don't do anything and Janet dies, and you're left with nothing but this book in your hands, how do you plan to live with yourself?" asked Cindy.

Whatever it was that was in the room watching them from behind David's back, bent close to him. Something urgent shaped itself into words which trickled in his ear: *Do it! Believe it! Do it! Do it!*

He covered his eyes with the palms of his hands and let out a long sigh. "Okay, okay," he said.

Diane put her hand on his shoulder. "We'll take it a step at a time, David," she said. "First thing in the morning we'll gather those herbs. Then we'll make the tea and drink some. Then, assuming it doesn't kill us or anything, we'll fill a couple of thermoses, sneak them into the hospital, and try to get Janet to drink some. And if it cures her, we'll know for sure."

"Yeah," answered David slowly, as if his mind were miles away. "It works pretty fast, according to Clayton." He stood up and stretched. His eyes were vacant, his brows drawn together. He wandered over to the west window and touched the night-cooled glass.

"Let's see—we want to leave for the hospital by eleven fifteen. Shall we get up about seven o'clock?" asked Diane as she stood up. "Where's

Clayton's herb book? I want to look up those plants. What were they called?"

"Vervain, Saint Johnswort, and bay laurel," said Cindy, yawning. "Take the book. It's on my bedside table."

David looked into the windy night and murmured, "Just think, she jumped out right through here."

"Come on, David, get out of here so I can get some sleep," said Cindy.

He backed away from the window. "I just wanted to see if the glass they put in to replace what she broke looked different from the old glass." He turned around. "Could I borrow that?" he asked, reaching for Clayton's journal. "I'd like to read it again before I go to sleep."

Cindy nodded as she gave it to him. "Library's closed," she said.

Diane laughed and kissed her, then pulled David by the elbow toward the door. As they were about to leave she said, "By the way, Cindy, you're amazing. Don't you ever get scared sleeping up here?"

"Nope," her little sister replied. "I've got friends to protect me. So do you, if you'd only pay attention to them. Now please do me a favor and let me get some sleep."

Chapter Twelve

White light blazed pain through Janet's eyelids. If she opened her eyes, her brains would evaporate and hiss away, like steam, through her eyeholes. Outside her skull, voices were chattering about things that had nothing to do with her. Inside her skull, she had left the tree that had supported her, turned her back on the corpse as it came towards her, and wandered away. She slogged through the thick, blackish-green waters of the swamp. The dead black trees were left behind and the waters had deepened and spread into a lake.

She knew that the corpse was following her. She could hear the slow splash of its footsteps. By wandering away, she had set it free from the plant-flames. Now, in return, it would free her from her suffering.

She was waist-deep in the water before she reached the wooden dock with the little white boat tied to it. With her last bit of strength, she climbed into the boat and stretched onto the bottom.

She heard herself say she was sorry to the boat. It was so white and she was so filthy. But she could lie down and close her eyes at last. The corpse was coming nearer. It would untie the boat from the dock and she would float away, away from the blazing light and the chatter and the pain.

The vicious splashings came close, then stopped. The corpse stank abominably, but she could forgive it. Lying relaxed on her back, she heard the wooden dock creak. There was a fumbling noise and the wheeze of dead breath through a broken windpipe. She heard a light thud next to her head as something flopped around in the bow. Then a grunt and a shove, and the boat moved away from the dock.

She knew that this was not a lake but an ocean, and the tide was going out. The boat moved swiftly. All she had to do was lie still and let it carry her away from the pain.

She heard the water splash against the sides of the boat. Then she heard many voices singing. The melody was irresistibly beautiful. As she listened, the headache began to ease. The great bubble of pain broke gently into smaller bubbles. She invited the singing to come closer. The more she welcomed the singing, the lighter the headache became.

Then, amid the singing, she heard that woman's voice speaking again, from right inside her ear. That deep, merry, ironic voice, and this time the words were clear. "Wait a minute—not so fast.

Hold on, hold on. There's no need to disappear yet." Sharp as a knife came a slice of fresh air and the smell of herbs, a pungent, woodsy smell that cut through the remnants of pain and stink and confusion.

The music began to fade.

Something from outside jostled her. Her nostrils flared to take in more of the smell. The headache broke up into tiny droplets. She breathed out and it was gone. The beautiful singing was gone too, but she didn't mind because now the chattering voices around her made sense. They belonged to people she loved and they were exclaiming, "It's working! It's working! She's waking up!"

She tried to sit up in the bottom of the boat. An arm went around her shoulders and helped her. She blinked her eyes open—and there was Diane, with tears in her eyes, watching her eagerly. The white boat was not a boat but a bed. The arm around her was David's. He was hugging her tightly against his old tweed jacket. In his other hand he held a plastic cup, from which curled the pungent steam that had awakened her and he was saying, "Drink this, Jan, can you?"

He held it to her lips and she sipped it. With each sip, she saw the world more clearly. Energy and common sense returned and, best of all, her head was free of pain.

She drank until the cup was empty. Diane took it and David hugged her again, carefully because of the needle which was inserted in her veins.

"Where am I?" she asked. "What are you doing here? I thought you were in Washington."

"We got back last night," said David, kissing the top of her head. "This is Saturday. You've been in here since Thursday morning. Oh, Janet! Ten minutes ago we thought you were dying!"

Janet relaxed in his embrace. "I'm amazed," she said. "I have no idea what's going on or how I got here, and I don't even have the words to ask questions. All I know is, I'm glad to see you and it's great not to have a headache."

Diane pulled out one of the thermoses she had in a bag by her feet, refilled the cup, and passed it to David. "You'd better drink some more if you can," she said to Janet. "Pretty soon the nurses will come in and when they find out you've miraculously recovered, they'll flip. Your mom and dad will be back in a little while too," she continued. "Your mom has been here the whole time. She slept on the cot there. When we got here, your dad was already here, so we suggested that he take your mom to get something to eat. That gave us a chance to get this tea into you. We didn't know how we were going to do it. I was thinking of dumping out the intravenous bottle and putting the tea in there. But as soon as you smelled it, you woke up."

"This tea is weird, but it's really good," Janet said, swirling the dregs around and looking into the cup. "It makes my brain feel like a crystal ball. What is it, anyway? And how did I get here? I want to know everything. The last thing I remember is—" she stopped, frowned, and leaned back against David. "Not pleasant," she said. "I don't like what I remember, not at all."

"Don't talk about it," said David.

"No, no, it's okay. I want to. I was in your house, in the conservatory, and there was this—this—it looked like a dead body, wrapped in a black cloak. It had chased me in there, and it was standing in the doorway stinking unbelievably and saying things like I'd be out of the way soon and then it would have *him*, forever. And I smashed a window with the stepladder—oh, no," she said. "I broke your window. Is your dad very upset?"

"Don't worry," David told her. "Your dad got it fixed by the time we got back."

"Oh good. My headache was so bad and I was so scared. It's all very dim but I must have gotten home somehow. Then, everything turned into a nightmare. This corpse chasing me—yuck, it was horrible. Is there any more tea?"

Diane reached down and brought up the second thermos.

David said, "I'll have some more myself."

As they drank, David and Diane looked at each other across the top of Janet's head.

"Well, what do you think?" asked Diane. "So far, everything Clayton said has checked out perfectly."

David nodded, but he turned down the corners of his mouth.

"Clayton? How'd he get in here?" asked Janet.

"Well," said Diane, "to make a long story short, it looks as if your life was saved by Cindy and two or three ghosts."

"No kidding?" said Janet, completely serious.

"I'm ready to believe anything. I want to hear all about it. And I'm hungry. I must not have eaten for days. When is somebody going to take this thing out of my arm so I can go home?"

Just then, the door opened and a nurse looked in, gasped, and disappeared. They heard her footsteps running down the hall.

"Here it comes," said David. "'Medical Profession Amazed by Miracle Cure.' Better put away the tea, Di."

A minute later, the room filled with doctors and nurses, all raising a hullabaloo. In the middle of it, Janet's parents walked in and added their gasps of surprise. Dr. Briggs, the doctor in charge of Janet, examined her from head to toe.

"Well, I must confess," he drawled as he scratched his forehead, "I've never seen anything quite like this before. It's truly remarkable."

"What is it, doctor?" Mrs. Gray asked.

"She's fine," he murmured. "Not a trace of anything wrong. Her pulse is fine, her breathing normal, her eyes couldn't be clearer, and her color, well, she almost looks as if she's been walking out in the woods all day . . ."

David and Diane winked at each other.

"This is astonishing," Mr. Gray murmured. "I mean, only last night . . ." his voice tapered off.

"Yes, hmmm, well yes, I know what you're thinking. Janet, what I'd like to do is have my colleague Dr. Harris take a look, if you don't mind."

"Then can she go home?" Mrs. Gray asked hopefully.

"Well, you see, Mrs. Gray, that's just it. I don't see any reason why not. The girl seems fit as a fiddle. That's why I would just like for Dr. Harris to have a quick look . . ." his voice trailed off as he scurried from the room.

Within seconds, Dr. Harris arrived and after a thorough examination, pronounced Janet to be one hundred percent better. "It is truly a miracle," she said as she nodded at Dr. Briggs. I don't see any reason why we should keep her here another night. There certainly are a lot of people who need this bed more than this young lady does."

David and Diane had to put their hands over their mouths to stifle their screams of joy. Within minutes, Janet appeared in the lobby of the hospital, attended by a candy striper pushing her wheelchair. All the way down in the elevator, Janet protested that she could walk perfectly well. The candy striper was about to explain that hospital rules said she had to use the chair but before she could do so, Janet jumped up and gave Amy a hug. Cindy stood by her side. Ever since Cindy had shown Amy the journal, the two had become best friends once again.

Although the doctors had suggested that Janet go straight to bed, she convinced her parents that David, Diane, and Cindy should eat dinner with her. "I really have to talk to them," she said.

"But Janet," Mr. Gray protested sternly. "You've just come home from the hospital. Surely you must be tired. I really think you should rest. You can always see them tomorrow."

"I know, Dad, but it's really important," Janet

persisted. "In fact, you could say that this was the most important day of my life. I really do have to talk to them now."

Mr. Gray turned to Mrs. Gray, who sighed and shrugged her shoulders.

"Okay, honey," he conceded, "but I still want you to go to bed early."

"Thanks, Dad," she said as she kissed him on the cheek and winked at her sister and three friends.

Chapter Thirteen

After supper, Janet heard the whole story. While David held her hand and Diane and Amy snuggled close by, she listened to Cindy read Clayton's journal. When it was over, she buried her face in David's shoulder and cried for a long time.

"Am I ever glad you're all here," she said as soon as she could talk. She pulled handfuls of tissue out of its box and blew her nose. "Now I'm really scared, not to mention disgusted. I wish I hadn't heard all of that. But I had to know the truth, didn't I? I wouldn't have slept tonight anyway, wondering what that thing was that chased me. Poor Clayton. Poor Vera."

David held her. Diane said, "But if their ghosts are around watching us the way Cindy says, think how happy they are. Remember, Clay swore they would come back and see to it that Margery gets what's coming to her. We did what he said and it worked. The tea cured you and now you're safe."

"I'm not sure how safe she is," Cindy said, "I'm glad she's out of the hospital because if Mirella found out she was there, she could have gone in, pretending to be a friend, and pulled the same trick she tried with Vera in the carriage. At least she's protected here at home."

"I'll protect you Jan," said Amy.

Diane nodded. "The sooner we come up with a plan, the better," she said. "None of us will really be safe until she's done away with. Once she finds out Jan's been sick and recovered, there's no telling what she'll do."

"And we have to be especially careful not to let her find out about the tea, or she might kill herself and get away again," said Cindy.

Diane asked, "I wonder if she has supernatural ways of finding things out? Does she look in a magic mirror or something? I mean, what if she's sitting across town right now watching us in a crystal ball, overhearing everything we say?"

"Oh come on, Di!" David burst out angrily.

"What's wrong with you?" Janet asked him. She had been watching him while the others talked. He frowned to himself as if something were seething inside of him. In his eyes she saw the shadow of a look she recognized and didn't like.

"Oh—" he said, "it's just—I don't know. I just don't like this talk about doing away with her. It seems so crazy. I mean, sure I believe Clayton's story. It's wild, but how could I *not* believe it after what happened today? But maybe it's not Mirella. She's a person like us. Why talk about her as if she was a wicked witch in a fairy story?" He paused.

"It's not that I like her especially," he went on, defensively. "I don't, even though I admit I did kind of fall for her at first. But just because you don't like a person is no reason to accuse them of being a monster."

"But David!" said Diane. "That's just what Clay and Cathy thought! They thought Margery was a normal human being. That's her disguise, that's what she counts on, that's how she fools us!"

"Well, what gives us the right to destroy her?" he asked stubbornly.

Cindy stood up. "David! you're being a total jerk."

Janet pulled out of his arms. "Amy," she said, "could you do me a favor and get me a towel?"

"Sure," said Amy. In a second, she returned with a big blue bath towel. Janet draped it across David's chest like a bib. "Now," she said, "where's that tea?"

There was still half a thermos left, lukewarm. Janet poured it into the cup and stood in front of David. Her face was set like a mask, white with anger. Calmly and gently, she tossed the tea at him so that it splashed on his forehead and dripped down over his astonished face. He sputtered and gasped, mopping his face with the towel.

"Did that hurt much?" Janet asked him.

"No," he said, "of course it didn't *hurt*—"

"He looks okay, doesn't he?" she asked the others. "No bones broken?"

"Just fine," said Diane.

"So what's the idea?"

"The idea is this. It didn't hurt you because

you're a normal, flesh and blood human being. That's what we all are, right? Who would die from a cup of tea over the head? But if what Clayton says is true, Mirella wouldn't even come into the same room with a cup of this tea, because she knows that if any of it gets on her she'll die. No— that's wrong—she won't die, and we can't kill her because she's *already dead!* We'll just be proving that she was never alive to begin with!"

"Oh," said David blankly.

Cindy said, "It's just like the old tests for witches, only backwards! They used to tie a big stone to a woman they had accused, and throw her in a well. If she drowned, they said it proved she was innocent, because· a real witch would have used magic to save herself. But with this test, if the tea doesn't hurt her, it proves she's not a vampire and if it does, it proves she is. So it's a fair test."

"And furthermore," said Janet, facing David with quiet anger, "if you are going to be devoted to her, you can keep precious Mirella, because you won't have me!"

"Jan," said David. "Please." He reached out for her but she just stood there.

"I'm sorry," he said. "I have been a jerk." He pulled Janet into his arms. For a minute she just stood there, not responding. Then she sighed and leaned against him.

"So," Diane said crisply. "It's decided. Let's make a plan if you're not too tired, Janet, or would you rather wait until tomorrow?"

"No, I'm fine," she answered, as she hugged

David. "I'll sleep better tonight if we've decided what to do."

"There's a little more tea left. Do you want it?"

"Give it to David. He needs it more than I do," Janet answered wryly.

They decided that Tuesday afternoon after school would be zero hour.

On Monday, Janet stayed home from school. The plan called for David to play up to Mirella, follow her around, beg to be allowed to carry her books, eat lunch with her, lend her things, pass notes to her in class, and in general, act smitten. Diane, too, was to be as friendly and sympathetic as ever and to make sure David didn't get carried away by his part of the game.

They brought a thermos of tea to school with them and swigged it to keep their spirits up and their wits about them. But after lunch, Diane noticed Mirella looking sharply at David. She pulled away when he went up close to her.

"I wonder if she smells the tea on your breath," she told him. "We're taking a big chance. Better not drink any more—if she gets suspicious, it'll be all over."

David made a face and agreed, but privately he wasn't sure he trusted himself. Mirella looked especially beautiful in a cornflower blue sweater with a gray scarf around her neck. Her skin glowed fair and flawless, her hair shone silkily, pale as moonlight, and her mythic eyes had a new expression in them—something almost playful.

When he first encountered her in the morning, he was taken aback by her loveliness. Then, remembering Clay and Vera and Janet, he sternly ordered himself not to be taken in. But as the day wore on and the tea wore off, the routine of school worked its own kind of spell on him. Mirella looked even more beautiful. How could she possibly be the gruesome creature they had all accused her of being? He began to feel almost protective toward her.

He knew perfectly well that he would never dump Janet for Mirella. She was inexpressibly special to him. No one could ever take her place. But as long as everybody understood that, what was the harm in a little lighthearted friendship, or even a little flirtation with another girl? Janet might be jealous of Mirella. He would be too, in her place. But why cook up a nightmare and subject someone to humiliating "tests"? It seemed slanderous!

School was out. He waited by the flagpole for Diane as he thought more about Mirella. He had just said goodbye to her and had looked into her eyes for one delicious moment, then, as he watched her walk across the schoolyard, he felt mesmerized by the swing of her long, full hips. She glanced back at him over her shoulder. Her raspberry lips formed the hint of a kiss and her eyes promised him something new—a new Mirella, a Mirella no one had ever seen before— and all for him.

He felt a sharp pinch on his arm and there was Diane, her eyebrows raised.

"Watch out," she said. "Don't take this game too seriously. Here." She unscrewed the cap of the thermos, poured some tea into it, and continued, "I think it's safe to have some of this now. We need it.

"It's strange, isn't it?" she continued. "I can see you're having a rough time and I really can't blame you. She looks so gorgeous today, so normal. It makes Clayton's journal seem like just ink fading away on crumbling paper."

"The past," said David, "crumbling to dust and blowing away, the way it's supposed to. I mean, it's a touching story, but in the first place, who knows if it's really true? He could have made it up. In the second place, what does it have to do with *us*, living people, going to school, driving cars, figuring out what to do with their lives?"

"That reminds me," said Diane, "I'll have to take the car to school tomorrow." She passed him the cup. "You know.

"Another thing I've noticed about Mirella," she went on. "I've talked to her, had lunch with her a bunch of times, and I've never heard her talk about what she's going to do after high school, whether she wants to go to college or get a job or what. She talks about two things—her hard luck story and you. It's as if her life revolves around you. She asks you all those questions and favors—it's as if she has to have you to navigate for her. I used to think it was just a way to get your attention, but maybe it's what Vera was talking about in Clayton's journal—she needs somebody else to live her life for her because she has no soul and can't function on her own."

David swallowed what was left in the cup and gave it back to her. "Yeah," he said. "It's true. She's a dippy one all right. That's what turned me off."

It was late Monday afternoon. Janet sat at the kitchen table and read to her mother from her American history textbook. It was the chapter she was supposed to have studied over vacation. She read it in a funny voice, making faces and gestures. Mrs. Gray rolled pieces of chicken in batter to fry for supper and laughed at her daughter. From the living room came the sound of the television which Amy was watching, as usual.

When the doorbell, rang, Janet abruptly stopped reading.

"Could you get that?" Mrs. Gray called to Amy.

Janet didn't move. On her face was a look of terror. She heard Amy open the front door and then a low-pitched, breathy, toneless voice said, "Hi! I'm Mirella, a friend of Janet's. I heard she was sick and I was worried. Could I come in and see her?"

"No way," said Amy. Her voice trembling and snappish. "She's too sick to see anyone."

"Oh, okay. I'll come by again tomorrow after supper."

"I really don't think you should," said Amy. "She's in bad shape. The doctor said no visitors.

When she's well enough, she'll call you."

"Oh. Well, could you please give her these, and tell her they're from me?"

"Sure. Thanks. Goodbye."

The door closed. Janet said, "Whew!"

Amy walked into the kitchen, carrying a bunch of white lilacs wrapped in tissue paper as if it was a dish of rat poison. "From Mirella," she said, wrinkling her nose.

"In the trash," said Janet as she looked the other way.

Amy took the flowers out the back door. Janet heard the lid of the trash can clang shut.

"Well, that's kind of a shame," said Mrs. Gray. "They were beautiful. Why did you have to dump them like that?"

"Because they were sent to me by my mortal enemy," said Janet. Actually, she thought, she's really my *immortal* enemy.

"Fighting words," said Mrs. Gray. "What's she done to you?"

Janet and Amy exchanged a look. "Well, for one thing," Janet began, "she's pursued David shamelessly, right under my nose." It felt good to be able to speak even part of the truth. "Bringing me flowers! What a hypocrite! I happen to know she hates flowers even more than she hates me. Thanks, Amy. You're fabulous. You get a medal for that."

"Any time," said Amy. She leaned against the refrigerator and looked at the floor. Obviously she wanted someone to ask her what was wrong.

"What's wrong?" Janet asked.

"Oh, just Mirella. She's so weird. I got the idea from what you've told me that she was ugly and wicked, and she *is* ugly and horrible—only she's beautiful on the outside. It makes the whole thing more horrible. When I look at her face, I get a stomachache."

That night, as David was entering his room, something made him hesitate in the doorway.

The bad smell was gone but now there was a feeling in the room that made him tense up. An exciting feeling, not unpleasant. Someone or something was waiting for him.

His eyes stretched wide open. He couldn't see anything because the room was dark, but when he reached for the wall switch, his hand stopped a few inches short of it, as if he didn't want to turn the light on for fear of driving away what was there.

But then he called himself a jerk and flipped on the switch. The big table lamp lit up and there was his room, all bright and looking the way it usually did: his bed unmade, his posters of Jupiter and Saturn on the wall, a heap of shoes near the closet door, his bookcase full of science fiction paperbacks and his old comic book collection, and his desk near the window, covered with textbooks and papers. And the feeling was still there. The light had neither dispersed it nor weakened it in the slightest bit.

He walked in, closed his door, and slowly went

over to his bed. He recognized the feeling. It was the same one that had crowded behind him the other night in Cindy's room when he was listening to her read Clayton's journal. Now it seemed to have intensified, filling the room. It was as if an urgent presence gathered together and concentrated directly on him.

Will you or won't you?

He took off his bathrobe, got into bed, and turned off the light. He curled up on his side and packed the covers firmly around himself.

He felt like a piece of paper under a burning glass, about to catch fire. Only these were not heat rays focused on him, but waves of urgency. Most maddening of all, they had a personal quality of their own. They were *somebody*, or rather, a combination of several personalities without bodies, all gathered around him, demanding something of him.

Are you going to or not?

He covered his head with the pillow, but that only made it worse. The presence—or presences, for they seemed to separate but combine and then separate again, like strands braiding and unbraiding themselves—was not put off a bit. It besieged him like an inquisition of invisible clowns.

Yes or no? Yes or no? Yes or no?

And then, inside his head, he heard someone laugh. A woman's deep voice. It was not his imagination. It was a real laugh, only it came from no mere human throat. It originated right there in the tiny chambers of his inner ear. And the laugh released something, a quiet flood of comfortable power, like an underground river, rich and dark, somewhat mournful from having been restrained so long. Its voice carried the voice that laughed in his head, just as any river carries its own bubbles. He relaxed, his eyes closed. The river was warm. He wanted to slide into it and let it take him away. Its voice sang in his head and asked him calmly, *Shall I live or die?*

He gave in. He went to the river, and the presence never left him. All night long it watched him. Wherever the river carried him, the presence went, too.

Toward morning, the river carried him into a dream. He was at school, in a class. The school was in ruins. There was no roof, sky-and-tree-filtered sunshine mingled with the fluorescent light from ceiling fixtures, attached to nothing. As for the floor, its square gray tiles were torn. Dead leaves and twigs littered it and collected in drifts along the walls. Saplings and new green grass were pushing their way up through it. In each corner stood a great big tree. The walls of the room ran into the trunks of the trees and blended so smoothly with them that you could hardly tell where the wall ended and the tree trunk began.

The walls were cracked and crumbling. The windows were paneless gaps with big chunks bitten out of the edges. Vines crawled in through these gaps and spread bony patterns over the insides of the walls.

The desks were the old-fashioned kind, where each one was welded to the chair-back of the one in front. They were rusted and falling apart, tilted at odd angles.

The classroom was full. There were a lot of people David didn't recognize. It was a geometry class. Mr. Mason was there, teaching them how to prove something. The blackboard was new and perfect, the only object in the room that wasn't broken. Mr. Mason was wearing brand-new glasses. When somebody commented on them, he said quietly, "Well, it's time I learned to see straight."

Sitting in from of David was Mirella. She turned and gave him a radiant smile. She had never looked more beautiful. When she faced the front again, the moonlight shimmer of her hair dazzled him. It hung gleaming down below the edge of the desk. He hadn't remembered her wearing it so long. It might even touch the floor. He couldn't help himself—he reached out and touched it, gathered it into his hand, and lifted the mass of it gently. Strangely enough, it didn't weigh anything. Milkweed was heavier. She tipped her head backwards toward him. Her hair and entire scalp slid off her skull and hung, floating in his grasp.

Her bare skull glowed, smooth and gray with greenish patches, like lichen. She swivelled it slowly around and smiled at him again. Her face was like a plastic mask fitted cleverly over the front of her head.

"Oh David," she said, "could I borrow a piece of paper?"

She held out her hand and when he looked at it, his stomach jolted. Her forefinger was infested with maggots. They were working their way down into the pad of her thumb.

He wanted to shift her hair from his right hand to his left, so that he could tear a sheet of paper out of his notebook, but when he tried to get a firmer grasp on it, it evaporated. His hand closed on itself—an empty fist. Yet the sensation of its weightless, silken flow remained on the nerves of his palm.

All throughout the dream, the presence remained close around him.

The river carried him out of the dream and up toward Tuesday morning. He landed gently on his feet and opened his eyes. The morning light was clear and steady in the room. His clock would ring in five minutes. Through the windows, he could see the treetops shining in the sun.

The feel of Mirella's hair still flowed across his palm. When he recalled her fingers, his stomach jolted again. He was thankful to be awake. But he felt as if he had never gone to sleep The presence had been constant throughout the night, accompanying him out of his dream like a special escort.

And it was still here, as strong as ever. *Well, will you? Will you?*

"I've no choice!" he said, throwing the covers aside. "All right!"

The tension around him eased at once, as if the escort had backed away. And when he came back from his shower, it had departed entirely.

Still following their plan, Janet stayed home from school that day, too. Word was out that she had been in the hospital, and people began asking about her. David and Diane shook their heads, looked serious, and said she was still pretty bad. They avoided telling their friends anything specific but the secret looks tossed to each other confirmed what they already knew—that today was indeed their only chance to carry out their plan. The deceptions were piling up. The strain was becoming unbearable.

As David went through the day, vivid images of last night's dream kept coming to him, like burps after a bad dinner. Feeling strained and unreal, he continued pretending to pursue Mirella. She looked ravishing, in an exquisitely sloppy way, wearing designer jeans and an oversized sweatshirt. Her hair shone, her skin glowed, and her dark eyes seemed to have little lights in their depths. She walked along close to David, never losing an opportunity to slink into the circle of his arm. And every time he took her hand, he tasted his dream and remembered how her finger had been sculpted of living fly larvae.

His face smiled, his eyes were directed at Mirella, his hands forced themselves to touch her. And his heart was a drum, steadily beating a march toward doom.

He knew that people disapproved of what he

was doing. Close friends looked at him oddly. Janet was seriously ill, they thought, and here he was fooling around with Mirella, giving in to her so easily. They must be beginning to despise him, he thought, and they were right to.

And he missed Janet. Suddenly, he missed her terribly—her intelligence, her humor, the way she would ponder and then say something insightful about what life would be like in a thousand years. In a flash, he remembered their first conversation by the brook. It was at that moment that David knew Janet was the girl for him.

The day wore on. Biology lab. French. Geometry. Lunch. He had to eat with Mirella, but Diane joined them so he had some help.

After lunch he sat through English, drama, and study hall. At last it was time.

Is this really going to happen? thought David. He stood beside the flagpole, watching Mirella come down the front steps. He felt trapped, exhausted. He couldn't believe he was really about to do the thing he had to do. He would have liked a belt of tea to fortify himself, but they had decided it would be too risky to bring any inside of the school. He'd have to do it all on his own steam.

Here she was, snuggling her arm through his and looking up at him. "Hi, David! What a gorgeous afternoon!" she breathed into his face. "Where are we going?" She gave him her books to carry.

"Oh, I don't know," he said. "Maybe someplace different." Trying to make his voice and manner seem casual and spontaneous, he left the school driveway and headed diagonally across the wide lawn that set the school building off from the road.

It was a perfect afternoon. So far, the sky had been cloudless. Now, from the west, long transparent streaks scrawled a titanic calligraphy across the stratosphere. The birds were singing and the soft new emerald green grass was sopping with golden sunshine. David wanted to take off his shoes. If he had been with Janet now, he would have.

He looked at Mirella. She walked fastidiously, as if the feel of the grass were not pleasant to her. Still, it was exciting to be alone with her, so close to the shimmer of her hair and the creamy velvet curve of her cheek. His pulse quickened. He felt confused.

When they came to the highway, David turned opposite to the way he usually went home. Mirella jumped over the ditch at the edge of the road as if she were relieved to get pavement back under her feet.

"It's so nice to be with you, David," she said, taking his hand. "I have a lot of trouble getting close to people. Nobody seems to like me. You're the only real friend I have."

"That's ridiculous," said David. "Everyone likes you. Diane does, and—and—and so does Annie, and Ronnie and Ed do—lots of people."

"Yeah, but it's different with them. It's just casual. They say hi and smile, but they don't let me get close to them. It's almost as if they don't trust me." She was almost whispering. He had to bend his head even closer to catch what she was saying.

"You know what really hurts?" she said. "The way Janet treats me. She *hates* me."

Oh, no, thought David. How am I supposed to handle this one?

"She does, she does," said Mirella as if he had protested. "I can tell. And I try so hard." Her voice was quivering.

Oh please don't cry, David thought desperately. I might not be able to stand it.

"I try to be nice to her, but she always backs away as if she's afraid of me. You know what happened yesterday? I knew she was sick so I went to visit her and I brought some flowers. Her sister answered the door and told me the doctor said Janet was too sick to see anyone. And that I shouldn't come back. She didn't even ask me to come inside or anything."

"Hmmm," said David.

They had already come almost half a mile away from the school. Without interrupting Mirella, David turned with her off the highway and they began to climb the hill toward a small glen.

"So I asked her to give Janet the flowers and she did take them. But then as I was leaving, I followed the road around the corner of their house, and I could see through one of their windows. I saw Janet's sister go into the kitchen. Janet was right there, sitting at the kitchen table, and she didn't look sick to me."

"Well, I don't think they're sure if what she has is contagious or not," said David. "They probably didn't want you to be exposed to it, in case it's catching."

"Oh? That makes sense, I suppose. But why didn't they say so? Anyway, there's more. I could see Janet's sister take the flowers into the kitchen and show them to Janet, and Janet looked the other way." The husky voice was quavering. "And her sister went out and put them into the trash can."

"You're kidding!" exclaimed David, genuinely shocked. "I can't believe it! Mirella, that's terrible."

"It's true," she whispered. Her head was bowed. She began to sob. David was dumbfounded. He had never seen her express so much emotion. "Doesn't that prove she hates me? And they were so beautiful—white lilacs, I cut them myself. Why are we going this way?"

"It's nice up here, you'll see," said David, pressing her along. "We'll have a little peace and quiet. What a shame." He had never been able to stand seeing people's feelings hurt.

She looked up at him. "Oh, David—" she burst out. This miracle of sophistication and self assurance was suddenly showing a heartrending vulnerability. "Everyone's against me—all my life, everybody's been against me. I try and try, but it doesn't do any good. I've always ended up alone . . . you're the first person who's ever really been nice to me. You're the only one who bothers

159

to understand how I feel."

David felt his heart cave in. Suddenly he wanted to stop, to hold her, to kiss and comfort her, to heal every pain she had ever suffered.

The shadows were quietly spreading themselves on the floor of the woods. Nearby but invisible, a wood thrush began singing its evening song. The sunshine was beginning to turn orange. David tightened his arm around Mirella and kept walking.

They had almost come to the top of the hill. Across the stream was a little footbridge leading to a path which crossed the hilltop. David led her over the bridge. She followed willingly, and went with him along the path, too. But when they had climbed a little further and she saw what was ahead of them, she hesitated.

"What's this?" she whispered, staring at the low stone wall, the old iron gate, and the gray troop of drunkenly tilted headstones beyond.

"It's an old cemetery," said David. "It's nice. A lot of these stones date from before the Revolutionary War—wait, these are bugging me." He set their books down on the stone wall. "We'll pick them up later. Come on, I'll show you."

But she hung back, clinging to his arm.

"You're not afraid, are you?" he said, with genuine tenderness. "Don't you know I'll take care of you?"

"Will you, David?" she whispered. "Oh, will you?" Tears spilled from her big dark eyes. Sobs tore her breath into heavy chunks. "Oh, I'm so lonely."

He felt her arm around his waist. She held him with amazing strength. Her shoulder under his hand was hard and tough like stones held together with wire.

"Nobody knows how lonely I am," she said. "Nobody's loved me. They pretend to, but then they always leave me and there I am, alone again. It's like a cold wind inside me."

They made their way slowly among the gravestones. The new grass brushed their legs. It seemed to make Mirella shudder, perhaps because it was cold with dew.

The wood thrush sang, sweet, cool, clanging. It played games with its song and sent out phrases, like queries, then it waited, then turned the same phrase inside out, waited again, then sang it a third way . . . like making different cat's cradles out of one loop of melody, David remembered Janet saying.

They crossed the graveyard. How tightly Mirella was holding him—her body was pressed against his side and her arm felt like an iron hoop around his waist. Was he still leading her or was she leading him? Perhaps it didn't matter. They walked together towards the northeast corner of the graveyard, where two headstones stood side by side, tilted towards each other. They were splotched with patches of gray-green lichen.

"These are the stones I wanted to show you," David said, and his voice shook. "They're very old. You can hardly read the writing on them."

But she was sobbing so hard he didn't think she could hear him. Suddenly, his own eyes filled up with tears and pity and remorse swelled in his throat and swirled like a gray mist in his mind. Through it, a familiar voice said, "Be careful!" but he paid no attention. Mirella's astonished misery enveloped him. Such a beautiful person, he thought, should never be lonely. How could anyone want to destroy her? Comfort was what she needed—comfort and shelter and healing. He wanted to give her those things. He wanted to prove to her that he could be trusted.

They stopped and faced each other. They were standing right between the two gravestones. Her face was as pale and lovely as a gardenia. The sound of her sharply indrawn breath pulled him closer to her.

"David," she whispered, "you're the only one, the only one who's ever really loved me. Please, please, never leave me. Promise. Say it—please. You're all I've got. Say you'll never leave me."

He took her in his arms. In his head the voice said something, but the words were drowned in the sweet dark tide of pity that surged up over his mind.

Of course he would give in. Of course he would save her. His lips parted, ready to whisper the promise.

Her face almost glowed in the dimming light. The ripe, trembling lips began to smile: her misery was turning to joy. In the depths of her dark eyes, something ignited. A pale flame was writhing. Her arms reached up around his neck.

He felt her hands on his head, her fingers

sinking into his hair. She was pulling his head down. How strong she was! Why did she pull so hard? She must know she didn't need to. She must know how much he wanted to kiss her.

She was holding him so tightly he could scarcely breathe. Her mouth was there, waiting for his. A whiff of something cold, ancient, and rotten made him try to pull away, but he couldn't She was too strong. He could only go one way: toward the lips that were waiting, opening, showing teeth . . .

A heavy splash, tepid and aromatic, fell around them. A gargled roar of outrage and anguish from Mirella. Another splash, and another and another. Mirella's face contorted. It was collapsing. She wailed and writhed and broke into pieces between his hands. An eye-stinging stench arose, as if a capsule of filth had burst. David jumped quickly and wrenched himself free of the arms that gripped him. They broke off and fell to the ground, slithering out of the sleeves of the sweat-shirt.

The smell of the herbs broke the cloying syrup of false pity and rinsed his senses clean. He stepped away and saw that Mirella's face was tipped back at a grotesque angle. Her head was sinking between her shoulders. The roar had split her throat wide open. The flesh of her face and neck was gone—dissolved into slimy grayish strands and patches which loosely clung to her bones. Her skeleton refused to hold her up. Within its clothes, now as meaningless as a scare-crow's, it buckled and the joints came apart.

David stood in his wet clothes, staring.

A thin gray soup drained out through the holes and crevices in the skull and sank into the ground with a faint bubbling noise. Pale wisps of her hair lay wet around the skull.

David felt numb. He wondered if he could walk. He tried a few steps. His balance was a bit shaky, but otherwise he seemed intact. Then his senses slowly began to come back. He looked around. He had had the feeling that night had fallen, but now he saw the sun was just going down behind the trees.

A few feet away, Diane and Cindy stood watching him. They were white-faced and seemed unsure whether or not to speak. Amy was off in the bushes, throwing up. Janet was taking care of her.

Janet. She had seen everything.

The whole hideous, shameful scene—how close he had come to giving in to Mirella, to betraying Janet, himself, all of them. Suddenly, David felt sicker than he had ever felt in his life. There was nowhere for him to rest his gaze. He couldn't look at the mess on the ground. He couldn't look at any of the people, those who had witnessed his great shame. If he covered his eyes with his hands, the images that flickered in the dark of his brain were too horrible to bear. He looked up through the treetops at the sky, which was void of everything, even of color, and it was as soothing to his eyes as cool water is to a tongue when it has been burned.

"David," he heard Diane say. She was putting a

blanket around him, trying to lead him away. "David, it's over. You're okay. You did it."

"Leave me alone," he said.

"Take it easy now. Here, have some tea."

"Tea! I never want to see the stuff again." But he smelled the aromatic steam and knew it was just what he needed.

Janet approached slowly, her arm around Amy. David looked away from them.

Diane filled two more cups with tea and handed them the brew. They stood together in a tight group, a few yards away from where it had happened, and drank. No one spoke. David still didn't look up.

Diane emptied her cup. "We have to go to the police right now," she said. "Leave everything the way it is. The buckets, everything."

They had used eight gallons of tea, in four plastic buckets. They had tried not to empty them completely, and left a bit in the bottom of each one as evidence.

"Let's go," said Diane.

They made their way among the gravestones and filed through the little gate. There on the wall were David's and Mirella's books.

"Wait," said David. "My books."

"Leave them," said Diane.

Over the bridge and down the hill they went, a troop of shadows in the twilight. The trill of crickets sounded all around them. Beside them on their left flowed the brook, almost invisible in the deepening shadows except for glints of the sky reflecting off its dark brown surface.

All the way down the hill, nobody spoke. David kept away from Janet. He couldn't bring himself to look at her or touch her. He felt filthy.

Diane had parked the car beside the highway, past the entrance to the cemetery road and around a corner, so David and Mirella wouldn't spot it when they came walking along. They got in— Diane in the driver's seat, Amy and Cindy beside her, and David and Janet in the back. Diane started the motor and turned on the windshield wipers for a moment to clear away the film of dew that had collected.

It was twilight, when your eyes are changing their way of seeing and you're not sure if you need your headlights or not. Diane switched them on and turned the car toward town.

Amy broke the silence. "Wow," she said. "All I can say is, I'm glad that really happened and wasn't a dream, because a real thing only happens once, but a dream can happen over and over again. Besides, I'm not even afraid of having bad dreams about it, because no dream could possibly be as bad as that." She paused, then added, "I don't think I'm even afraid of dying any more."

Janet reached over the back of the front seat and touched her sister's head. "How are you feeling?"

"Fine," Amy answered.

David shivered in his wet clothes and looked out the window. He hated himself. He wished Janet were not there. How could he ever look her in the eye again? She made no move toward him, either. Just as well, he thought.

A mile or two went by. He stared out at dark trees, lawns, houses, other cars. He resigned himself to despair, and began to savor its bitterness. It was silent in the car. He wished he really was alone. Then he heard Janet move, and felt her hand in his hair, then on his cheek. He wanted to resist, but couldn't. He allowed his head to turn and he met her eyes.

She looked into his eyes deeply with such matter-of-fact tenderness and acceptance that a smile started in the depths of her eyes. He felt tears rising in his own. "David," she said with a smile in her voice, "it's okay. It had to be that way or else she wouldn't have gone along with you. We couldn't have gotten at her if you hadn't really almost given in."

He couldn't stand it. He looked away. She turned his chin making him face her again. Really smiling now, she kissed him. He pulled her to him and felt her shake with laughter.

"What's so funny?" he said into her ear. He still felt more like crying.

"Well," she said, "at least you're finally convinced!"

He gagged. "Am I ever!"

She stopped laughing and kissed him. "I'm proud of you," she whispered. He drew her to him again and hid his face in her hair. The shock of it all was getting to him. His shivering was becoming violent. He gave in to it and let her hold him.

The car slowed down and turned. They were in the parking lot behind the police station.

"Okay, everybody," said Diane. "Let's pull ourselves together. I think we're in for a long night."

The story the five young people told, supported by Clayton Dexter's journal, had a cataclysmic effect on the town. There were six weeks of searches, questioning, and investigation, inquests, and an autopsy. But no matter how long and hard everyone tried, they could find not one grain of evidence to either contradict or explain the incredible truth.

Mirella's foster aunt did not exist. Mirella had no birth certificate, no school records, nothing to justify her existence at all except for the coroner's report, which stated that the remains found in the graveyard were at least three hundred years old.

In the end, the townspeople just shook their heads. How could they believe the unbelievable?

One warm night in June, the scent of honeysuckle flowed in on the velvet air. Outside, in the darkness under the trees, the first fireflies replied to the candles on the Sperrys' great dining room table. The Sperrys, the Grays, and Mrs. Wiggins were gathered to celebrate. Mrs. Wiggins had given Cindy the portrait of Vera to express her gratitude at having the Dexters exonerated after so many years.

Three extra places had been set at the table.

Mrs. Gray commented on it when she walked in. "Why," she'd said, "aren't there only ten of us?"

"No," said Mrs. Sperry, "those three are for the guests of honor, who happen to be invisible."

"Ah," said Mrs. Gray, "of course. I should have known."

Janet gazed at the portrait all evening. When she had first walked in and seen it, she had gasped.

"That pink dress," she said to David. "I knew it—it *was* Vera I saw in the gallery on the night of your party."

The longer she looked at Vera, the more readily the tears came to her eyes. There she was, dead, and yet she had saved Janet's life. Dead, and yet so fiery and sweet, gazing down upon them as if she would have liked nothing more than to join the party.

"Oh, Vera has been around all along," said Cindy. "I knew. I felt her the strongest of all of them. I couldn't tell anyone, though, because you would have said my imagination was running away with me."

At the end of the evening, Mr. Sperry stood up, holding his glass of brandy, and said, "I want to propose a very special toast to the health of our invisible friends, with thanks to them for showing us that if you have a choice, it's much better to live among spirits who have no bodies than among bodies who have no spirits."

"Here, here," said everyone. Glasses clinked.

Suddenly, everyone gasped. As Mr. Gray

touched his glass to the three glasses that had not been raised, a puff of blue fire appeared in each and played over the surface of the brandy.